Neri, Kris,
1948-

Revenge of the gypsy
queen.

$20.00

DATE			

A Rainbow
Mystery

Revenge

of the

Gypsy Queen

Kris Neri

Revenge
of the
Gypsy Queen

—A Tracy Eaton Mystery—

RAINBOW BOOKS, INC.

Rainbow Books, Inc.
P. O. Box 430
Highland City, Florida 33846

Copyright © 1999 by Kris Neri

Library of Congress Cataloging-in-Publication Data

Neri, Kris [DATE]
    Revenge of the gypsy queen : a Tracy Eaton mystery / Kris Neri.
    p. cm.
    ISBN 1-56825-043-6 (alk. paper)
    I. Title.
PS3564.E64R4   1999
813'.54--dc21   99-22401
                                                                        CIP

ISBN 1-56825-043-6
First Edition 1999
Printed in the United States of America.

For Joe,
the music of my heart,
my soul,
my life.

ACKNOWLEDGMENTS

Gratitude goes to the members of my sometime critique group, Susan Casmier and Larry Hill, for their guidance and nurturing of my various drafts; and to Suzanne Epstein and the gang in the SinC/LA Writers' Support Group for their encouragement. Barbara Lakey, the editor of *Futures*, gave me the tip that sent me to Rainbow Books, Inc., for which I'll always be appreciative.

Thanks go to Detective George Nagy of the NYPD for helping me to understand the workings of the New York Police Department, and to G. Miki Hayden for patiently answering my New York questions. Joe and Siri (aka Elizabeth Dearl) Jeffrey gave me the lowdown on long-range rifles, cheerfully answering endless questions, for which I'm grateful. A great many cops and others from around the country also answered my questions anonymously online. Thanks to everyone who helped me to uncover facts; however, all choices and errors are mine alone.

To borrow a few words from the heroine of this book, I find that I've devalued superlatives too much for them to adequately express the profound debt I owe to some: my husband, Joe, for never losing faith that this day would come; Ruth Sydney Segel, for always believing in me; and Betty Wright, publisher of Rainbow Books, Inc.

REVENGE
OF THE
GYPSY QUEEN

PROLOGUE

Talk about the unexpected. I came to New York for a vacation and to share in the joy of my sister-in-law's wedding. The operative word was *fun*. Instead, I wrestled with extortion and murder — not to mention losing ten thousand bucks — and I hadn't even been on the subway!

But I'm getting ahead of myself. During my first full day in New York, I had no inkling of the ugly obstacles that would rear up on the road ahead, though I'd already gathered it would take a few surprising bends — thanks to a rather strange and wonderful afternoon.

During my return to my in-laws' Upper East Side townhouse, my mind reeled with questions: Why were the police watching my husband's Uncle Philly? What could that lovable cherub, whom I wouldn't trust as far as I could throw Manhattan, have done to attract the attention of the boys and girls in police blue? And if Philly interested them so much, why didn't the cops haul *him* in for questioning — instead of *me*?

Not that the afternoon was without its compensations. I considered getting tossed in the hoosegow as nothing less than the attainment of a merit badge I'd coveted for years, as well as priceless entertainment. Especially when it provided a little family dirt my in-laws obviously didn't want me to know.

But dampening the experience was the unease I felt over the one question that really mattered. The question that had gnawed at me since my sister-in-law, Marisa, failed to turn up for our appointment that morning: What had happened to her? Where was Marisa?

I'd hoped no one would be home; I needed time alone with my thoughts. No such luck. Both my husband, Drew, and his mother, Charlotte, pounced on me the instant I entered the townhouse foyer. I noticed not a hair of Charlotte's honey blonde head was out of place, but there was fire in her stormy blue eyes. Was it too late to make my escape?

"Tracy! Finally, you're here," my mother-in-law said with an impatient sniff. "You're the only one who has seen Marisa today. Perhaps you can tell me why she hasn't kept any of her appointments."

"Actually, we never — "

The telephone rang.

"Doesn't that phone ever stop?" Charlotte's rhetorical demand overflowed with aggrieved righteousness. "Drew, I am not your sister's answering service!" she snapped, as if it were his fault, before dashing to the den to answer it.

It troubled me that they hadn't seen Marisa, either, but they weren't supposed to. My rational mind continued to override the doubts with its insistence that Marisa and I would share a good laugh over the mix-up before the evening ended. Sure we would.

Drew and I strolled arm-in-arm past the staircase and

into the living room. I noticed one lock of his wavy light-brown hair fell over his forehead, the way it did when I played "Tracy and the stable lad" in my head. But his golden eyes looked glazed and irritated. Must have been jet-lag.

He took me into his arms. "Mrs. Eaton, I hope you feel just a bit guilty. Gallivanting around while I've had a miserable day."

"Really, Mr. Eaton? I'll have you know my day wasn't all fun and games, either."

Emphasis on the word, *all*. The games I played with Philly and Detective Billy Jay Weaver were worth the price of admission at police headquarters.

"No contest," Drew said. "I had the pleasure of my mother's company when she learned my sister has fallen an entire day behind on the wedding schedule."

So those tired eyes were the result of Charlotte-stress, not travel-fatigue. Much worse. My first glance at the room should have told me. Charlotte always kept her home ready for an impromptu *Architectural Digest* spread. Sometimes I half expected to be cautioned to stay behind the velvet ropes. Tonight, while the room tastefully decorated in this season's selection of greys still had a long way to go before looking lived in by anyone else's standards — for this crowd, it was downright messy. The black jacket tossed on a chair would have been bad enough, but the heather grey scarf that had slipped to the floor was unforgivable. The blizzard of neatly printed Rolodex cards scattered on every surface practically signaled the end of the world.

"And *you* had to be late," Drew went on. "When my mother wanted to question you about Marisa, and I assured her you would be home early."

"Why did you do that?" I demanded in self-defense.

"Because you left me a note saying you wouldn't be late."

As a mature adult and an officer of the court, Drew has a penchant for justice — which means he's a stickler for apportioning blame. And he operates under the ridiculous idea that I sometimes try to get out of things.

"Drew, it's your fault that I'm late," I said.

He threw his head back and laughed like he'd needed a good one for a while. "How do you figure that?"

I snuggled closer to his stiff-as-a-board white shirt; the Eatons might feel a little rumpled on rare occasions, but their clothes would never tell. "Your cloak-and-dagger game started it all. It was only because I saw you following your uncle that I did, too. By the way, what's Philly's last name?"

I noticed the man in the circle of my arms was pulling away from me.

"You're mistaken, Tracy," he said, as if he spoke the unvarnished truth.

"About his name? If you don't tell me things, how can I be wrong?" I complained.

"I meant, I wasn't following my uncle. What gave you that idea?"

"Drew, I *saw* you. You sailed right past Marisa's very own restaurant in a cab."

"Must have been someone else," was his airy response.

"I know my own husband!"

"Obviously, not too well. I haven't left the house all day."

His eyes met mine and stuck with all the might of

Krazy Glue. He believes that to be a sign of honesty. Like he would know. Drew is the world's worst liar. With his strict ethical code, he doesn't get enough practice. He was making up for it now. If things got any screwier around there, I was going to need a guide.

The doorbell rang once, then a couple more times in rapid succession.

"Marisa!" I said. "Probably just forgot her key."

I heard a flood of relief in my own voice, far greater than the level of anxiety I acknowledged. I ran to the foyer. Before I reached the door, the ringing gave way to an insistent pounding. Suddenly, I knew Marisa and I weren't going to share that laugh tonight, after all.

I stopped, unable to take another step, unwilling to face whatever waited on the other side of that door. I'd always held in contempt the people who avoid the tough stuff. But I'd engaged in denial about Marisa's whereabouts all day. I clung to it even now.

If life hadn't already taught me about the price of silence, I would learn it when I opened that door. And I would pay that price for as long as I lived.

1

I should have known the whole trip would take a detour through Wonderland, considering how it had started.

There I was at the airport check-in counter back home in Los Angeles, locking eyes with the clerk, but he stubbornly refused to ask The Question. He did ask the others. He said, "First class or economy?" and "Window or aisle?" He just wouldn't ask whether we insisted on air that — apart from being recirculated since the dawn of time — was more or less fresh, or if we preferred to be surrounded by compulsive personalities puffing on dead weeds.

Domestic airlines don't have smoking sections any longer. Naturally, I knew that before I reached the check-in counter, despite the stupid look I'd plastered on my face to hide my dismay. I just keep hoping they'll change their minds.

Not that I smoked. Filthy habit. I haven't had a cigarette now in three months, twenty-two days — and I'm not so pathetic as to count minutes, but at a guess, I'd put it at forty-one and a half. So why did I shove yet another stick of gum between my tightly clenched teeth when I heard they didn't have a place for something I didn't do?

What can I say? I kicked the habit; I just couldn't kick the enjoyment I derived from catching the odd whiff of the secondary killer.

But I was holding up well. I was just so focused on the clerk, certain at any instant he would rectify his omission, that I didn't realize the woman in line behind me had addressed me the first time she spoke.

"My dear," she repeated with a hint of impatience, "I *said*, did anyone ever tell you that you look like Martha Collins, the actress?"

Aren't voices funny? If you hear them before seeing someone, they never match. This woman sounded young and girlish. But judging by the *spots de liver* that were so thick they might have been painted on her hammy hands, she was never again going to see the sunny side of seventy.

Smiling modestly, I said, "I should look like her. Martha Collins is my mother."

"Though you are a bit more substantial," she continued, as if I hadn't spoken. "Martha Collins is so hauntingly ethereal."

Was she calling me fat? She should talk. She might have had that small voice, but this woman was built like a brick company latrine — to be delicate in my description of her.

"What did you say? You're her *daughter*?" she asked, catching up. "Of course. You're little Tracy Grainger. I remember seeing pictures of you with your parents in *Life* magazine. I so wished I could dress my girls like you, but they were older. I had my children a lot younger than your mother."

Who didn't? There was probably a whole minute left

before the shutdown of Mother's reproductive system when they conceived me. It's a wonder I turned out as normal as I did.

She raised a delicate hand to her mouth to cover what promised to be a ladylike clearing of the throat but which emerged as a cough that was more in line with her mammoth frame. Then she politely extended the hand that had trapped that honker within her. "By the way, I'm Mrs. Thomas Dodd."

"I'm Tracy Eaton now," I said and shook her hand like the true sport I am.

"Married." Mrs. Dodd gave Drew an approving glance. "Children?"

I shook my head.

"Don't wait too long, dear. Remember, in those pictures in *Life* your mother was no longer the ingenue."

But she was ethereal.

My good fortune held. Mrs. Dodd enjoyed our chat in line so much she snagged the seat next to me on the plane. A five-hour flight with Drew on the aisle and Mrs. Dodd in the window seat. Lucky me.

" — so I visited my married daughter in Los Angeles. And they took me everywhere, honey, let me tell you."

She told me.

"I had such a good time, I decided to visit my other daughter in New Jersey."

New Jersey? I thought, listening against my will. Someone should have told the old dear that Newark was a closer airport than Kennedy.

"Traveling is wonderful," Mrs. Dodd said, "but when it comes to a place to live, give me Bakersfield every time."

I wouldn't dream of taking it away from her, even after hearing her recitation of its many virtues.

"Are you going to read your flight magazine?" Mrs. Dodd asked. "They didn't put one in my seat."

There wasn't a flight magazine for my seat, either. I snatched the one Drew was reading right from his hands and gave it to her.

"Hey!" he shouted.

"Drew, she *wants* to read!" I sang in the tone previously reserved for the announcement of the realization of world peace.

But she didn't want to read it, merely to use the rolled-up magazine as a prop for her re-creation of the stunning performance King Kong gave on the Universal Studios Tour.

I was too excited to care. There I was on a flight to New York to attend the wedding of Drew's little sister, Marisa, my favorite relative.

If Marisa didn't bear some resemblance to her mother, I would swear she'd been raised by wolves rather than by a family in the Social Register. Not that she wasn't an absolute sweetie, but she was dramatically different from parents who didn't favor deviations from the norm. She was as attractive as all the Eatons, but exotic to their all-American, creative to their conventional.

No one objected when Marisa developed an interest in cooking, but when that led to an entry-level job in a commercial kitchen, the parental howls should have been heard in Alaska. But they never uttered a peep. Perhaps they were simply humoring Marisa, allowing her a job unsuited to the uptight, upright Eatons, while waiting for the interest to pass. But they had to know that was unlikely to happen when, after returning from an elite Italian cooking school, she and her new Italian fiancé, Tony Lora, opened their own restaurant, The Gypsy Princess. I never understood how she pulled it off, nor why Drew couldn't do it, too.

"Did you hear that?" someone asked.

It was Mrs. Dodd, ruffling my reverie. "The movie. The stewardess said they can't show the movie; the equipment is broken. Can you beat that?"

No movie. Be still my heart.

The flight passed. Word by word. Well, I did wrestle the conversation away occasionally. Like when Mrs. Dodd actually asked me a question.

"So, Tracy, what kind of work do you do?"

With one eyebrow intriguingly raised, I said, "I'm a detective."

Drew was chewing one of the airline inedibles at that moment. He nearly gagged.

Can you blame me? Hadn't this woman read anything since one issue of *Life* magazine in 1970? Everybody knows the daughter of Hollywood legendaries, Martha Collins and Alec Grainger, writes the Tessa Graham Mystery Series, even those louts who limit their reading to Hollywood scandal sheets. If she didn't, her chain was ripe for yanking.

Besides, what I said was nearly true. Or would be eventually. That was the bitter irony of my life. While in my work I struggled to invent plausible reasons why my character, a scholarly professor, tripped over bodies continually — the only mystery in my real life was why two newspapers were delivered to my neighbor on coupon days, while I never received any. Nothing intriguing ever happens to me. In books and movies, when someone writes about an amateur detective, people assume she can solve crimes, too. Mysteries just fall in her lap. But my first case would come along any day now. Not today or tomorrow, naturally, but soon.

You should have seen Mrs. Dodd. An uncomfortable smile tugged at the corner of her mouth, now slack with shock. People often laugh when they find themselves in situations beyond their emotional depth. Obviously, I was too far off the mean for this country granny.

She didn't say a word. Not how exciting, how dangerous, how whatever. She just plunged into a graphic recital of the childbirth sagas of every member of her family. I wasn't even sure they were all female.

Well, I might have claimed a bit more of the conversation than that. I probably relayed the entire family's plans for those pre-wedding weeks, my concerns about my matron of honor gown, a detailed description of the elegant decor of my in-laws' home, my speculations about my sister-in-law's intended, as well as several thousand other thoughts that flashed through my mind. I talk when I'm excited. I talk when I'm depressed. When I'm awake, when I'm asleep. About the only time I don't talk is when my mouth is full, and I'm very slender. Damn near ethereal! I just hate competition.

Mrs. Dodd wasn't that bad, as seat mates go. Before we parted, she remembered to return the flight magazine that neither she nor I, not to mention Drew, had read, and she left me with a few words of wisdom. I should ease up on the makeup as I approached my mother's age and be sure not to forget, during these hustle-bustle weeks, to eat my roughage.

I felt like warning her to watch her own health. When we parted, she let another one of those consumptive coughs fly. Not so much as a whiff of smoke came off her clothing, but I sensed she was another recovered tobacco addict, though she had obviously played Kentucky Roulette longer than I had. I wouldn't have pegged the old dear as the smoker-type, but it just goes to show you that people will fool you every time.

2

Mrs. Dodd must have carried on her luggage. I didn't see her in the baggage claim area. But the fun still wouldn't quit. I sat on one of our suitcases, wondering whether checking them in at different times would make them come up together, while watching an empty baggage carousel go 'round and 'round.

Next time, Scotty, *beam* me up.

To stifle the boredom and catch up on what was happening in New York, I opened the copy of the *Daily News* I had the presence of mind to buy when we passed through the terminal. The lead story about the indicted mobster, John Anthony Briachi, was filled with as much sensationalistic innuendo as I remembered, but the unflattering photo of his fat, ugly face achieved a new low. I loved it.

Naturally, I'd keep that thought to myself. Briachi was not a man to joke about. From what I'd heard, his exploits made the horse's head scene in *The Godfather* look like a party game. Now the Justice Department had him up on a list of charges as long as his arm. The contention that he was the biggest drug distributor on the Eastern Seaboard was one of the least significant.

I glanced up to monitor Drew's progress. It was easy to pick him out, since he wore his stodgiest grey pin-striped suit. Such a good little lawyer — who visits his parents dressed like that? Anyway, there were maybe a whole six passengers still waiting for their luggage. I was about to return to my paper when something happened to jerk the rug out from under my blasé sophistication.

"Drew!" I said in a reverent hush as he delivered another bag to me. "Look. Over there! No, don't turn around. She'll know we're talking about her."

"Then how — "

"Make it casual. Then look over there."

"Where, Tracy?"

"There!" I said, pointing in exasperation. The things he makes me do. "It's Zoya Vrescu!"

"Who?" the ignoramus asked.

"Zoya Vrescu, the ballerina."

"Which one?" he asked.

I indicated inconspicuously this time with a subtle toss of my head.

"Surely," Drew concluded, "that's *retired* ballerina."

The boor. Of course, she was retired. She had to be well into her fifties now, and no one bounces around on her toes at that age. But Zoya still looked the quintessential ballerina. Slender as a girl, she moved with a dancer's magnificent carriage. She was an exotically handsome woman, especially with her black hair pulled back into the classic chignon. Actually, she'd pulled it so tightly, it was a wonder her dark eyes didn't look out from her temples. But irrepressible waves still made slight indentations all over her head. Her hair must have been really curly.

"I can't believe we were on the same flight — and I didn't know it," I said with a groan.

"Tracy, you're star-struck. When I think of the way you put down the fans who gush over your parents, I can barely keep from laughing."

From where I stood, he surrendered without a fight.

"Drew, you don't understand. Zoya Vrescu gave me my first moment of real enchantment. When I was five years old, I saw her dance right here in New York, and it was — " For the first time in my garrulous existence, I was speechless. After a lifetime of extravagantly squandering superlatives, I now found them too devalued to describe that magnificent experience. "I was supposed to see her again a year later in London, but she canceled her European tour."

"And that was the greatest disappointment of your young life?" Drew asked, not unkindly.

"Just about," I admitted.

What I didn't tell him was that I hoped to follow her into the ballet, only the required talent never developed. While I loved my life, even now, as I watched that exquisite woman glide across the floor, surrounded by a fawning entourage of college boys, I felt a tinge of regret.

"There's my suitcase." Drew dashed to the carousel.

Star-struck? I thought with indignation. How could I be star-struck? Besides possessing some prominence as a writer myself, I was born to a pair of full-fledged celebrities. My life had been spent mingling with the world's notables: Heads of State, religious leaders, royalty, all the major diet book authors. Hollywood luminaries and I had always been on a first-name basis. Renown didn't impress me — I knew those people put their pants on one leg at a time. When their dressing room keyholes were large enough, I watched them do it.

But Zoya Vrescu . . . Okay, so maybe I was star-struck. Can you blame me? It was funny that I hadn't met the one celebrity that mattered most. If I'd attended that ballet with my parents, we would have gone backstage after the performance, but they were tied up with their own show. That matinee was a gift from their secretary, a former dancer herself, who generously shared her knowledge and appreciation. I'd always been grateful for the experience, but I wondered fleetingly whether my life would have been different if I had known the great Vrescu.

"Here's the last bag," Drew said when he returned to my resting place, dragging his huge, overstuffed suitcase behind him. "Did you find a porter?"

Was he talking to me? "Can't you carry them?"

I thought I heard some miscellaneous swearing from his direction, but I couldn't be sure, since I was moving through the door. Men. You know you've been married too long when he no longer needs to show you how strong he is.

I was sure Zoya Vrescu had walked out of my life, but her entourage was even slower than we were. Drew and I had already taken our place at the end of the taxi queue when she floated past us. I freely forgave the inviting smile she offered my husband despite the twenty-odd years she had on him.

"Look," I said, "that must be her limo."

Drew rolled his eyes. If he thought I cared that I sounded like a drooling adolescent fan faced with the latest bubble gum heartthrob, he was wrong. Besides, their idols were just manufactured images.

"Probably rented," Drew said.

"With that license plate? No way."

So I was inconsistent. Sue me. I knew if anyone else flaunted that personalized plate, I would have dismissed the act as arrogant. What can I say? For Zoya, it worked. The outrageously accurate plate read:

STAR 1.

A desperate need to follow her surged in me, thus removing any doubt the word *fan* was derived from *fanatic*. The adult within me overcame it, as I made peace with the image of my idol driving out of my life. Besides, my shoes were killing me.

Hey, if I really wanted her address, I could always pry it out of the Department of Motor Vehicles. I couldn't say how strenuously the State of New York guarded the privacy of its drivers, but it's a point of honor with me that I can get anything from anyone.

That thought must have found its way to my face. Suddenly, Drew looked as comfortable as a bird at a cat show. With his rugged movie star jaw and dimples I could curl up in, Drew was a major hunk. Not a bad bod, either; the view from behind was not to be missed. On the downside, he was stiffer than steel. Sure, I forced him to bend a little on occasion, but as soon as I let go, he tightened up again, especially when his parents entered the picture. How could someone his age still need to please Mommy and Daddy, and how could they expect it? A mystery to me, but admittedly, my parents and I were all a little fuzzy on our respective roles.

"Uh — Tracy, you are going to behave yourself on this trip, aren't you?"

Behave myself? You'd think I was a two-year-old being cautioned not to pee on Santa's lap.

"Of course." My smile could have caused cavities. "Don't I always?"

I love it when he turns that color.

Drew surged forward when we reached the front of the taxi line, while I dawdled behind. When I caught up to him, he was stalled at the curb waiting for the cabby to emerge from his cocoon and stow our bags for us. At least he flipped the trunk latch, when he might have expected us to break it.

"I've been away too long," Drew concluded.

New York cabbies, God love 'em.

We settled back for the last part of our journey. Drew sucked air through his teeth when we lurched into traffic. He *had* been away too long. Though a native New Yorker, he'd become acclimated to the craziness of driving in Los Angeles, as opposed to the nuttiness of New York driving. The difference, as I saw it, was like that between warfare from a plane and hand-to-hand combat. Me, I could do battle anywhere.

Once we were on our way, I spread my paper across my lap to finish reading the article on Briachi. "Ah, New York, New York. Such extremes. Where else would you have a brush with both a ballerina and a mobster?" I asked, forgetting for the sake of literary license that the only brush I was ever likely to have with Briachi was from the newspaper.

Drew smirked. If he thought I cared that he was above my slumming, he was wrong. Why would I want to share my paper?

"Anyone can make these fake combinations," he said. "In Southern California we have actors and coke dealers."

"How can you call that a fake combination? They're often one and the same." But I grasped his point. Vrescu and Briachi weren't connected except in my experience. As if they could be. Now that I thought about it, I found I didn't want a scumbag like Briachi sullying my awe of Zoya Vrescu. I'd read about him later.

I stuffed the newspaper into my tote bag, along with the flight magazine Mrs. Dodd had returned to me, and pressed my face to the glass to study the sights and sounds beyond the windows. I felt great. The brush with my childhood idol recharged the excitement traveling had sapped.

I couldn't wait for this vacation to start. It was going to be a wonderful time of shopping and shows and pre-wedding fun, balanced out as everything must be — or it would be too, too great — with some Quality Time with my mother-in-law. Nothing earthshaking, just an ordinary, family occasion, though the stuff from which memories are made.

And I called myself a detective. Some people wouldn't recognize the start of a case — if it bit them on the fanny.

3

Ah, families — can't live with 'em, can't kill 'em.

We had gathered around my in-laws' rich mahogany table, which reeked of lemon oil polish, for a sumptuous meal the engaged couple, in a rare night away from their restaurant, had prepared for us. The white linen place mats gleamed brightly against the dark wood, and the Waterford glasses sparkled with a rainbow of shimmering colors in the chandelier light. Amid fresh fettuccini Bolognese cooked to a perfect bite, to-die-for rosemary focaccia bread, and the best ossobuco this side of Milan, we were the picture of togetherness.

"It's beyond me why any man would consider the *institution* of marriage," Drew's older brother, Corbett, said. He punctuated the remark with a long swallow from his glass of Brunello di Montalcino, the exquisite red wine we were enjoying this evening.

It was the third time he'd expressed that belief, though he enunciated it more exactly now as he was a sheet or twelve to the wind.

"It's all skew — skew — geared to the woman," he spat out, sending a fine spray of wine spittle in a wide circle, spoiling the linen before him.

Charlotte's hand jerked slightly in a reflex toward the salt.

My father-in-law, Taylor, viciously tore a piece of bread that he stuffed into his mouth, while gazing warily on his first born. At the other end of the table, Drew tapped his fingertips against the table in time with the vein throbbing in his temple.

Corbett seemed oblivious to those signs of anger. While clearly cut from the Eaton mold, he lacked his mother's poise and his father's charisma, and with his thicker features, Corbett wasn't as attractive as Drew. On the other hand, he was drunker than all of them combined.

"Guys don't stand a chance. But are they grateful? Not on your life. Bunch o' un'preciative leeches," he went on.

"Corbett, haven't we heard enough of this?" Drew held his brother's eyes in a steely lock for a moment, before looking away. "Will somebody pass me the grated cheese?"

Corbett grinned and gestured to Drew with his glass, tossing ruby drops of wine which beaded on the polished tabletop. "Your turn will come, buddy-boy."

It wasn't hard to figure the source of his tirade. Corbett's wife wasn't with us this evening; some months before, that well-bred socialite took off with the twenty-two-year-old guy who cleaned the pool at her health club. Since I hadn't seen much of my brother-in-law in recent years, I wondered whether his behavior was the result of his wife's abandonment — or the reason she left.

"Sure," Corbett went on. "Your turn will come."

"Just so long as the cheese does," Drew said.

Marisa handed Drew the bowl of shredded Asiago

with a stifled giggle. They bit the insides of their cheeks to keep from laughing. I might envy the camaraderie siblings shared, if the other member of this trio hadn't just reached across me and grabbed the wine bottle by the neck.

Charlotte alone seemed determined to ignore her son's graceless display. She took a ladylike bite of pasta and closed her eyes as she chewed, as though in prayer. "Exquisite, as always, Tony," she said, for which she received a humble nod from her future son-in-law.

But Corbett refused the reprieve. "What do they want? Huh? What do they want?"

The questions weren't rhetorical. He looked at each of us in turn, as if he were granting us a long-sought chance to defend womankind in general. The process stopped when he reached his mother, which it would have anyway, since she was the last woman there, but perhaps not so abruptly. I never noticed before, but Corbett had developed his scowl at his mother's knee.

An unusually pretty blonde, Charlotte loved being told she looked too young to be the mother of grown children. It might have even been true, if she could loosen up. But she was the most tightly controlled human being I'd ever met. I swear, the Queen of England was less anal about protocol. Her teeth were so tightly clenched now, I thought her eyes would pop.

Trust my father-in-law, Taylor, a vintage version of Drew, to come to the rescue by diverting her interest, though I questioned his juggling of frying pans and fires.

"Tracy," he said with a wink, "it's a shame your parents won't be here for the wedding."

I'd often suspected Taylor's easy charm shared as much responsibility for his successful legal career as his sharp mind. At times, he showed such engaging wit, I found myself wondering if there wasn't another Taylor, a side he revealed only at work, where he was a senior partner of a Wall Street law firm. The man with that knowing twinkle in his eyes couldn't possibly be the patriarch of this conventional brood. Then I looked at the signature button-down shirt and his old prep school tie, which I suspected he wore even while playing golf, and I knew these were his people.

"A tragedy," Charlotte purred too sweetly. Well, who could blame her? The last time her path and Mother's crossed at a wedding, Charlotte left with a black eye.

But she sure was getting catty. I remembered what happened when we arrived that afternoon.

∞

"You'll never guess who I saw at the airport," I announced within moments of my arrival. "Zoya Vrescu!"

"Who?" my sister-in-law, Marisa, asked.

Didn't anyone in that family know anything? "Zoya Vrescu, the ballerina."

"Is she still alive?" Charlotte asked, her voice shrill. "At her age, you'd think — "

I never did learn what you'd think about an age that might have been a smidge younger than Charlotte's.

"Charlotte," Taylor said.

Okay! Tension. I would not have thought a foreign dancer and a WASP socialite had much of a twain on which

to meet, but all sorts of women do committees. Whatever happened between those two must have been a doozy.

I couldn't let it go. "Do you know her, Charlotte?"

"We've met — but no less than a lifetime ago."

I heard the ring of honesty in her voice. Go figure.
She used to apply her claws more sparingly. Fortunately,
not all the Eaton women were that nasty.

∽

"It *is* a tragedy that your parents won't be here," Marisa
insisted.

"They're sick about missing it, but at their ages they
can't pass up leads in a movie, even if they have to go to
Russia to shoot them."

Well, they would be sick about it, if they knew. I must
have staked out their mailbox for a week before I managed
to steal the invitation. They'd be furious when they learned
I robbed them of the chance to come. My parents adored
Marisa. "The girl's the only sane one in the bunch!" Dad
bellowed after the meeting of the families, proving how
standards change when the inmates run the asylum. Still,
that wouldn't stop their marauding egos from destroying
her wedding.

I bent my head toward my plate so no one would see
how smug I felt about averting that disaster. I twirled a
final forkful of fettuccini with great panache and stuffed it
into my mouth, chewing slowly to make the flavor last.

"By the way, Tracy," Charlotte said. "Martha left a
message for you."

My head flew up, and the meat sauce I'd swallowed

threatened to make a return appearance. "Here?" I asked in a squeak. "Did she say what she wanted?"

"You know Martha. She just babbled on. Something about Alec flirting with the script girl. What did she expect you to do about it from here?" Charlotte asked.

Drew's fork slipped from his hand, hitting his mother's precious Spode with a clang, and he shot me a look that said, *Say it isn't so.* He knew my family well enough to interpret that message. Mother was going to demand that I skip the wedding and fly to Moscow to settle the latest dispute between her and Dad. The harassment had already begun. She might have been cheated out of making an appearance here, but that didn't mean she wouldn't make her presence felt. It was anyone's guess how far she would take it.

Drew reached for his wine and nearly knocked the glass over. Once it stopped rocking, he clutched it in two hands and took a fortifying gulp.

"You'll call her back, won't you, Tracy?" Charlotte asked, before taking another tiny bite.

"You know, I will," I said with a serene smile. When pigs sing the blues. If I avoided Mother long enough, she would tire of this game and go off on another shtick. Hopefully, one that victimized some other poor bastard.

"You sure have a colorful family, Tracy," Corbett said around a mouthful of focaccia.

"Amen," Charlotte agreed. The dainty pat she gave the side of her mouth with her napkin looked so superior, I wanted to hit her.

Naturally, I never argue with drunks and women whose hospitality I need. But that summed up the difference between this family and me. They all seemed committed to leading lives lacking in color. Literally, sometimes. I nearly choked when I came to dinner and found most of them dressed in black. I thought I'd stumbled into a funeral. I'd forgotten how much chic New Yorkers love wearing black. Well, cool Angelenos wouldn't be caught in anything else at their Saturday night clubs, either. Not me. The fuchsia silk suit I wore tonight was so bright, Charlotte kept looking away from it, as if it burned her retinas.

While I scraped the last of my sauce from my dish with a big hunk of bread, a *faux pas* at that table, I stole a glimpse at Marisa's intended, Tony Lora. I wondered how well he was coping with this show of family solidarity. If he'd even followed it. With his heavy Italian accent, it was anyone's guess how much he understood. During the worst of Corbett's ravings, I caught Tony watching his almost-brother-in-law with mingled emotions reflected on his expressive face. Compassion, but also something that looked like frustration. It has to be tough when someone doesn't understand the language well enough to express himself.

When everyone had eaten down to the pattern on their plates, Tony rose to clear the pasta dishes, while Marisa served the main course. I liked watching them work in unconscious harmony. They looked good together, though in a beauty-and-the-beast way. Marisa was tall and slim and moved with the grace of a runway model. She had dark, curly hair — not the soft, light brown waves Drew and Corbett shared with their father — exotic almond eyes, and her mother's attractive smile. Or what would have been her mother's smile, if Charlotte ever loosened her jaw.

It wasn't fair to call Tony a beast; there was such an

appealing quality to his homeliness. On a body just this side of gaunt, his craggy nose, which would have been large under any circumstance, appeared to slice the air a foot in front of him. Some people wouldn't trust a chef who wasn't heavy, but only if they viewed food merely as sustenance. To Tony, I suspected, it was the canvas of his creation. Maybe it was the artist's passion that gave his humble face its character, but I believed it was his eyes. They seemed too sad, too aware of life's darker side to be part of the same person who created this incomparable meal. There were unexpected quarters hiding within this silent stranger.

I wondered how he and Marisa communicated. Did she enjoy teaching him English or find it a strain? Maybe she appreciated the disinterest it gave him. Sometimes you need a referee.

"By the way, Marisa," Corbett said, as he dug into his ossobuco, "I forgot to tell you. Hunt made another offer for your restaurant the other day."

Marisa, poised to place her napkin on her lap, hurled it instead at the table. "Damn you, Corbett. You're supposed to tell me the instant you hear anything. You better shape up, bro, or the co-op, not to mention The Gypsy Princess, is going to find another lawyer."

I touched my ossobuco with my fork. The meat fell from the bone. I took a small piece and just held it in my mouth, letting my taste buds identify every single herb. Did I groan aloud?

"Go ahead — fire me," Corbett shouted, his face flushing with the vibrant glow too much booze imparts. "I don't need your lousy job."

We were swinging at each other again. "Hunt who?" I asked to distract them.

Everyone stopped whatever they were doing — forks and glasses froze in midair — and they looked at me as if I had just dropped from Jupiter or Mars.

"*Lord* Hunt, of course," Marisa said.

Of course. Despite how it sounded, Lord Hunt wasn't an English peer. *Lord* was the outrageous first name given him by a mother whose grandiose delusions proved inspirational. If you were to ask, I'd bet most people in the country would probably name Hunt as the richest man in the world. In actuality, it was unlikely that he even fell in the top five. But that didn't mean he qualified for welfare. When the person bent on developing every square inch of urban America operated, it was with syndicates and leveraged-out holdings and massive loans; it was anyone's guess how much of the money was his alone. Though with that many zeros, what did it matter?

Considering how the tasteless, flamboyant Hunt courted the press, he was oddly reluctant to part with the few facts financial reporters really wanted. Like where he came from and where he found the seed money to begin his campaign of uglifying cities from coast-to-coast. Lord Hunt enraged his fellow New Yorkers more than anyone else, since his hometown was his favorite target.

So why would an empire builder want one little restaurant? I wondered, more than a little baffled. The Gypsy Princess, their Soho eatery, was a hot spot — but as anyone aware of the food industry knows, temperatures cool. I put that question to Marisa.

"Restaurants are a marginal business," Marisa admitted. "I know that too well. If we were only one restaurant, Hunt's interest would be curious. But he wants us because of the co-op." She gestured down the length of the table. "Mom, could you please pass me the veggies?"

While Marisa replenished her plate, she described the experimental restaurant cooperative of which The Gypsy Princess was a part. More than fifty privately-owned restaurants had banned together to save on expenses.

"We buy in mass, pool employees, and help each other. More than a few would have gone under in this competitive market if it hadn't been for the support of the other members," she explained.

"But Marisa, she is-a — how you say? She is on-a top of the co-op," Tony said in faltering English.

What do you know? So some Italians actually speak in that clichéd accent.

"What Tony means is that Marisa is the president of the co-op," Corbett said. "If The Princess knuckles under to Mr. Mighty, many of the others will fall, too. That's why he keeps making offers. He wants all the restaurants in the cooperative, but he knows the dam will break with The Princess."

I saw strength and conviction in my sister-in-law's clear, dark eyes. Hunt had chosen wisely — she would have to be the one to topple. But I still didn't understand his interest.

"Why restaurants?" I asked. "So you found a way to wring out another percentage point of profit. This game's ante still isn't high enough for the great Lord Hunt."

I tried the baby carrots and potatoes swimming in a delicate lemon-herb sauce. This was better than sex, though I kept that thought to myself; no one else seemed as close to orgasm. Too much impulse control.

Marisa shrugged. "It is hard to figure, but Hunt owns several national chains of family restaurants. I suppose this is the first time he's found a profitable way of branching into the upscale places."

"This wouldn't be happening — if you let your father and me finance your restaurant the way we wanted," Charlotte said. No orgasm there; it took her two bites to finish a one-inch carrot. "Your father has some standing in the financial community, after all. This Hunt-person wouldn't push him around."

With all due respect to my father-in-law's standing on Wall Street, I didn't think he was any match for a shark like Hunt. From the wary look on his face, neither did he.

"I thought you did finance it," Drew said. "I mean, I figured — " He stopped, burying his face in his water glass, probably when he realized how rude his remarks sounded. Unlike me, Drew considers nosiness an unattractive trait.

Taylor glanced at Charlotte and rushed to avoid another cause of contention. "We offered but were politely refused."

"We found another source for the extra money we needed," Marisa said.

"A silent partner they were sure would remain silent," Corbett added with a boozy giggle.

"As if we wouldn't," Charlotte said. This time all of her children kept a tactful silence.

Dinner went on in fits and starts, with enough smoothed-over tiffs and spats to make me glad I was an only child, though not enough to wish I'd been spawned in a test tube. It took my own parents to do that. Eventually, we mellowed out. It was probably Tony's sumptuous dinner that did it. Or Marisa's sinful Baileys Irish Cream tiramisù. Though maybe our drinking enough brandy to fill an oil tanker had something to do with it. By the time we pushed ourselves away from the table, we were finally having fun.

Then — it happened.

We didn't recognize it as the sound of doom, just the doorbell. But when Taylor returned from answering it, he looked like a guy facing a firing squad. In his hand he held an old-fashioned, yellow-paper telegram. I didn't know they still sent those things. The sight of it snuffed out all the laughter but mine.

It always amazes me that other people associate telegrams with tragedy. The only ones I'd seen were those my parents received when they opened in plays. Something told me, however, that I was alone in my belief that the sight of that yellow paper signaled the start of a happy event.

Charlotte's wide eyes found the yellow paper Taylor clutched. "Is someone — "

"Dead? No," Taylor said.

"Thank God." Relief filled my mother-in-law's words.

"It's worse."

"Worse than death? Really, Taylor," Charlotte snapped, but she looked worried.

"Charlotte, it's your brother, Philly." Taylor swallowed hard. "He's coming to the wedding."

I thought she would faint.

Ah, families — maybe you can kill 'em.

4

I stifled a yawn. Good thing the back seat of that cab wasn't too comfortable or I'd have fallen asleep on the spot. Four hours of sleep didn't cut it on a travel day. But I wouldn't have missed the events of last night for the world. Chaos entered the Eaton house as a first-time guest and stayed to rule the roost. Last I heard, it was still there, sleeping in the master bedroom.

My first thought when Taylor announced the contents of that telegram was whether anyone was close enough to catch Charlotte before she hit the hardwood dining room floor. I forgot about her superb poise.

"How ni-i-ce," she said, squeezing it out.

With that proclamation, her children and husband exhaled. I hadn't noticed before, but the room was too quiet for everyone to have been breathing. The Eaton kids' anxiety gave way to excitement, as they shouted out their favorite Uncle Philly anecdotes. Charlotte, meanwhile, looked collected, composed, smiled sweetly to each new chorus of "Do you remember when . . ." as she calmly decided what she would wear in the last hour of her life.

Needless to say, we would all have benefitted from

having a night's rest before the next round. Too bad. The arrival of Philly's telegram just barely allowed enough time for someone to pick him up at the airport. When I asked why he didn't take a cab, my question produced a variety of answers.

Corbett held an empty wine bottle over his glass to catch the drops. "He's probably just short of cash."

"U.S. currency. He won't have enough till he exchanges some," Drew added with grim determination.

Marisa snorted. "You mean he won't have enough till he wins more at craps."

Craps? This family played polo, not craps. They didn't know how to spell craps.

Charlotte just pushed her chair away from the table with a sigh and announced the arrival of a headache. After Drew and Taylor left, she went to her bedroom to rest. Tony generously offered to do all the cleaning up. Corbett volunteered to help, only he toddled off to the living room and stopped off at the sofa for a snooze.

Marisa hooked her arm through mine and led me to the den, my favorite room in that mausoleum. While the rest of the place was always designed by one of New York's stuffiest decorators, Charlotte put that family room together herself with castoffs from other rooms. Everything fit together, but not quite as well as the showcase settings, and that made me feel more at home.

It was the only place where it felt okay to tuck my feet under me, as I did when I sank into the cushy blue side chair. Though maybe the restrictions were all in my mind. Marisa had no qualms about kicking off her patent leather pumps and propping her feet on the coffee table, where she wiggled her toes to the extent her charcoal knee-highs would permit. Hell, at that moment, the family's eldest was probably drooling into the living room sofa cushions.

Tony made a quick appearance carrying a tray with a couple of steaming mugs topped with whipped cream. "I bring-a you *cioccolata*."

"Great, babe." Marisa rewarded her fiancé with a subtle smile that suggested a shared secret. A love of chocolate?

Hot chocolate made from scratch *and* homemade whipped cream — where do you find these guys? While we sipped our cocoa nectar, Marisa entertained me with another Uncle Philly story, the one that inspired her restaurant's name.

"I thought you just picked something catchy," I said.

"Great if it works that way, but the words *Gypsy princess* go back to when I was a little girl. One of the little WASP princesses I went to school with decided my appearance fell too far out of her blonde hair/blue eyes parameters and started calling me a Gypsy. You know what little bitches they can be." Marisa absently picked at an invisible spot on the sofa arm.

"Present company and your mother excluded, of course," I said, playing it straight. Caught up in the reminiscence, she was obviously unaware she had just described her two closest female relatives in less than glowing terms. I felt it my duty to bring it to her attention.

"Of course," she said with a nervous giggle.

When my uncharacteristically grave face cracked into a big grin, we both dissolved in a rush of uncontrollable laughter.

"Damn you, Tracy." Marisa laughed good-naturedly

and faked a swing at my arm. "Anyway, after that girl called me a Gypsy, everyone else copied her. Well, maybe just her followers, but that was enough. At that age, it's tough to feel different."

I nodded. "Some kids can be little skunks."

"Sure can. I told Uncle Philly about it, and he wove those words into a fable about a struggle between a beautiful Gypsy princess and an evil Gypsy queen. The queen tried to steal the sun from the princess; she wanted it to fill the cold, empty place within her. But the Gypsy princess was smart. She tricked the queen into showing her true colors to the king, who banished her to a place that was as cold outside as she was inside, while the Gypsy princess lived forever in the warmth of the sun."

"Happily ever after?" I asked.

"Is there any other way?" She plopped her mug on the table with a satisfied tap. "Isn't that a beautiful story?"

There were a few holes in the plot, but I admired the novel approach. Wicked stepmothers and Prince Charmings had been done to death. Perhaps evil birth mothers and Prin*cess* Charmings were just the kick in the pants the fairy tale world needed.

The den was the closest room to the foyer, but we both became so lost in Marisa's reminiscence that we jumped at the sound of the key in the front door lock. Uncle Philly was there.

While Marisa gathered the rest of the clan, I wandered to the foot of the stairs to wait. Since the arrival of that telegram, I'd witnessed an assortment of reactions to a man I'd never met. I based my image on the extremes of those reactions. I envisioned him as a womanizing urbanite, drifting through the gaming capitals of the world, existing on what Charlotte might consider "the wages of sin" as little more than a high-class gigolo. What other than amoral charm could send Charlotte through the roof while simultaneously captivating her children?

I could not have been farther from the truth and still been in this universe.

The man who stumbled across the foyer Oriental rug was rumpled, chubby, and cheerfully — no, proudly inept. His salt-and-pepper hair stuck up in pointy little tufts, and two or three days' worth of matching stubble covered the lower half of his face. I'd like to say his crumpled, brown-tweed suit had seen better days, but its days had never been good. He hadn't fallen quite so low on life's ladder as those people who sleep in bus stations, but he could reach down and touch them from where he was without stretching.

Now this person would have been right at home in my parents' house. Dad collects some odd friends, most of whom he picks up at race tracks and pool halls, though he also frequents less reputable haunts. But in this museum? I would have sworn no one who looked like Philly had ever entered this house.

Charlotte disappointed me. Sure, she was stuffy, but I never considered her a snob. But what other than social stature could she have against this sweet-looking man?

I found myself liking him. How could I help it? His version of the family smile, which he shared with his sister and niece, was the most joyous of the three. And the expression in his sparkling blue-green eyes was that of the boy in your sixth grade class whose spitballs always nailed the teacher's butt. Man after my heart.

Besides, no matter what impression his appearance made, Philly would have won my affections with the first whiff he sent across the room. Yes, whiff—I did mean the aroma. Back in the glory days when sensible people smoked, Dad enjoyed an occasional pipeful of Flying Dutchman tobacco. Drew considered it cloying. I wouldn't know; I couldn't judge it on merit. That scent would always resurrect the warm fuzzies I felt when I sat on my dad's lap and buried my face in his cashmere sweater.

Apparently, the regard was mutual. After Philly greeted the family, he swept me into a bear hug. "Tracy, honey, Drew was right. You're just as pretty as your famous mom." He went on to relay a few other things Drew had said.

Funny, he knew so much about me, while I'd never heard of him. I threw a questioning glance in Drew's direction, but he became absorbed in scrutinizing the dusky pumpkin paint on the foyer wall.

Eventually, the long evening had ended, but not before we batted around the sleeping arrangements. The house contained a basement apartment that once housed servants. Since the kids had grown, Charlotte no longer employed live-in help and had converted the apartment into a guest suite. I offered to take the smaller guest room and let Philly have the apartment. Charlotte hesitated. For once, I didn't think she was trying to make the proper hostess choice but debating whether she should give in to the desire to put her dear brother out of sight. She must not have found him that offensive, since she finally insisted Drew and I needed the extra space. I didn't argue; the suite was more private — and, boy, did we need to talk.

The guest suite was the one part of the townhouse in

which the decorator was obviously permitted to exercise her creativity. I bet she described that collection of blacks and whites and greys as "young" or "with it." At thirty-four, I just considered it funereal. I tried not to step on the cracks of the alternating black-and-white marble squares which made up the floor to save my mother's back.

The instant we were alone, I asked Drew why I'd never heard of his Uncle Philly.

"I don't know," he said. He strolled from the bedroom back to the sitting area.

I stalked him. "Andrew, perhaps I'm being too abstract. We're not debating metaphysics here. I'm asking why *you* never told *me* about your mysterious uncle." I looked to where Drew's eyes focused on the floor. Checkmate?

He mumbled something about it slipping his mind, which we both knew was absurd. There were no slippery surfaces in Drew's mind. It didn't look like I was going to pry any more from him, but I knew for sure when I casually asked about Philly's profession. Drew spent five minutes telling me why he couldn't delay going to bed a single moment longer, rather than taking an instant to answer my question. Very strange. Drew was never evasive. But this entire trip was providing unique instruction for those of us convinced we'd seen it all.

∞

Drew had been asleep when I'd left this morning, and we weren't able to continue the conversation. My guess would be Drew planned never to continue it. You'd think he'd learn.

I yawned again, and when the cab dove into a pothole, I only barely avoided dripping coffee onto my new forest-green linen pants. I'd better snap out of this. Marisa and I had a full day of wedding stuff planned, one we'd been scheduling by phone and e-mail for weeks. But I desperately needed caffeine. The Grande Cappuccino with Easy Foam I'd picked up at Starbucks before setting out hadn't begun to kick in. And if I came within grabbing distance of anyone with a cigarette, New York mugging statistics were going to rise. I was weak.

The cab driver let me off across the street from the exclusive bridal shop where Marisa and I were meeting to be fitted for our gowns. I couldn't wait to see my dress. Marisa had promised it would be something I'd be proud to wear again, but brides have to say that. Sure, I was tired, but I'd swear I looked up the street before crossing. Experienced jaywalkers always do, it's second nature. I remembered seeing that rusty grey van rolling toward me, but I judged it far enough away to allow me to sprint across the street before it. But as I approached the middle of the street, it accelerated. Faster, faster — it was coming right at me! Fatigue slowed my reaction time, robbing me of the split second needed to run from its path. My only chance was to hurl myself onto the hood of a Jaguar parked along the curb. And I only *barely* made it.

I know New York drivers like to go for the jugular, but usually it's just in fun. This woman really meant it!

Woman? Did I really have time to notice the driver? While I checked to see whether either the Jag or I needed body work, I ran my memory tape. The driver was a woman, all right — a large, redheaded woman. Stranger still was the odd sense of familiarity I felt after my brief sighting of the van's driver. How many people did I know in New York?

And why would one of them want to run me down?

5

Marisa hadn't arrived by the time the dressmaker finished my fitting. I struggled to hide my distraction when I assured the shop owner I loved the gown. No lie. It was a simple, icy-blue number with iridescent beading on the bodice. Beautiful enough to make me hope Mother would fight with Dad just before the Academy Awards again this year and invite me to go instead. Now I would no longer need to squeeze into one of her dresses, ethereal little thing that she is. But my heart wasn't into flights of fancy. It wasn't like Marisa to be late. While generally looser than the other Eatons, she did share their zeal for organization. Some crisis must have popped up at the restaurant. I went on to The Gypsy Princess, figuring I'd meet her there.

No dice. She hadn't gone in that morning. Tony said she'd had a few errands to run before meeting me and must have been delayed. Maybe she just misunderstood where we were supposed to meet. We decided she'd show up soon. Anyone responsible for running a restaurant, heading a cooperative, and planning a wedding was entitled to a little lapse, even if it wasn't like her.

Flushing with pride as he brushed his dark hair off his

broad forehead with his fingers, Tony gave me the grand
tour. Marisa had described the decor of The Gypsy Princess, but I hadn't seen it. With that buildup, I expected a
lot and was still impressed. Located in trendy Soho in the
loft of a refurbished commercial building, the restaurant
was a symphony of mocha, cream, and plum, with surfaces
of oak and glass and brass, and planters full of birds of
paradise and other exotic flowers, all awash in the light
streaming through huge skylights.

Tony encouraged me to drop in for visits while I was
in New York. He pressed a key to the rear alley receiving
elevator into my hand so I wouldn't have to wait until the
busy hostess had time to roust him from the kitchen. I
accepted the key to be polite, though I couldn't imagine
letting myself into a commercial kitchen. Someone might
put me to work!

Marisa still hadn't shown up by the end of the tour,
and Tony insisted I start my lunch without her. No argument there. I hadn't eaten any breakfast, and though the
adrenalin generated by my brush with becoming road kill
did a lot to overcome my fatigue, I needed fuel. I ordered a
chopped salad, but Tony wouldn't hear of it. In his atrocious English, he insisted on creating a special lunch just
for me. I couldn't refuse — it wouldn't have been polite.
His creation turned out to be garlic chicken ravioli in a
creamy pesto sauce. I knew I'd swallow every bite. Hell,
I'd probably lick the plate. But if I ate many more of that
man's meals, my gown was going to need another fitting.
So much for ethereal.

Since I'd planned for a full day, before leaving the house
I stuffed everything I could possibly want into the tan can-

vas backpack I carried. Including the flight magazine I'd taken from the plane. Drew always laughs because I can't bear to be caught anyplace without something to read. Came in handy this time, didn't it? I entertained myself while eating by reading an amusing article on the decline and fall of the human race.

But as the time passed, my unease about Marisa's absence filled me along with the food. Tony felt it, too — his strained expression told the story — though we lied to each other about our concern. He produced a phone, and we left breezy little messages for Marisa at their apartment and the Eaton townhouse. I knew we were both disappointed that she didn't pick up at either place.

Suddenly, I also found myself at loose ends, my tightly planned day having now unraveled. I could drop in at my publishing house, but with my editor out of town a visit didn't make much sense. I decided to do a little window shopping, something that's always fun in New York, and promised to touch base with Tony later in case — correction, *when* Marisa returned.

Puffy white clouds dotted a brilliant blue sky. It was a beautiful, late-September day. New York was enjoying the same weather we'd left behind in Southern California, balmy days and nights just cool enough to need a blanket and the arms of the one you loved.

When I paused on the sidewalk outside The Gypsy Princess to gather my sense of direction, something odd caught my eye. A man I'd noticed sitting in his car across the street when I arrived was still there, and I'd swear he was watching The Princess. Stranger was the sense that I'd seen him somewhere, though I couldn't remember where.

That feeling of seeing familiar faces in an unfamiliar place seemed to be wafting over me way too often. Something hit the sidewalk next to me. I looked up to see whether the ghost of Rod Serling was flipping butts at me. It was only a pigeon flipping you-know-what. All this *deja vu* was getting too weird.

The man apparently decided he'd seen enough; his black Crown Victoria jerked into traffic. Driving seemed an unfamiliar task. Or maybe he was just lousy at it. I watched him depart, alternating lurching and slowing; perhaps he should have started with a compact model. Then, I dismissed him from my mind. Why? I saw another face I recognized moving through traffic in a cab. Wasn't this the day for them? But this one needed no identification — it was my husband's.

With Drew still asleep when I'd left this morning, I hadn't had a chance to ask about his plans for the day, though I'd left a note describing mine in case he'd forgotten every mention I'd made over the last two months. Since my afternoon had just opened up, maybe I'd tag along with him. I flagged a cab.

"Follow that car!" I shouted to the driver.

I'd always wanted to say that. It must have also brightened the cabby's day; he got right into the spirit of things.

"All right!" my Middle-Eastern driver said in excellent English. "American detective-talk!"

See, even *he* could tell. He put my command into action. Fortunately, traffic was light — we jerked to a halt only every three or four feet.

"Miss?" the driver asked after a while. "Did you know the cab you're pursuing is following another cab?"

Drew was tailing someone?

"I also suspect the man in the first cab is trying to lose him," he said.

It didn't take me an instant to decide, but I debated whether my driver would go the distance. Like many taxis in these dangerous times, this cab had been equipped with one of those plastic dividers between the driver and passenger. But the divider had been broken off along its base. That allowed me a clear view of the driver's coffee-colored eyes in the rearview mirror. Was that a spark of fun I saw? It seemed to fit with the dashing handlebar moustache he wore. I found myself smiling into the reflected eyes of a kindred spirit.

"Stay with the first car. Don't let him shake you." Who could Drew have been following? Curiosity ruled my life.

This was great. I'd had so little fun from the time Mrs. Dodd plopped next to me on the plane, I was going into withdrawal. Now we were cooking.

Let the games begin!

My cabby was better at this than Drew's driver. Or perhaps he simply thought the fun of it offset the risk of a ticket, which I would have paid anyway. I lowered my head when we sailed past Drew's cab, lawfully stopped for a red light. Then we tailed the lead car through a series of erratic turns designed to shake anyone following. My driver varied his pace and his distance. His moves must have been good enough to allay the suspicions of the lead car's passenger. The evasive maneuvers stopped, and we were able to get close enough to learn the identity of the person we were tailing.

Philly.

Drew had been following his own uncle. I almost told the driver to turn back toward the house — until it dawned on me that Philly had deliberately shaken his nephew.

We were still headed downtown, and if my recollection of Manhattan geography was correct, we were going to run out of land soon. I'd go along with almost anything, but once we hit the water, Philly was on his own.

Not that I wasn't enjoying this. During one of those hopeless New York gridlocks that come and go without warning, the cabby told me his life story, which was really fascinating. His name was Nuri al-Barazi; for most of his life he'd been an architect for the Iraqi government. He'd secretly worked with the Allies during the tense days of Desert Shield but was discovered just before the start of the war. He'd been imprisoned until some of his friends managed to secure his release, and they helped Nuri and his family escape the country. But they'd lost everything. The Hawaiian print shirt he wore was strictly Salvation Army thrift shop quality, but Nuri brought some unexpected dignity to it with his confident bearing. Driving a cab might not be the kind of work he wanted, but for now, it was as close to the American Dream that the Barazi family could get. Fortunately, with his whimsical, ironic nature, Nuri seemed to be handling it well.

Philly's cab turned east. Nuri took his turn more slowly so it didn't look like we were following. Philly's driver turned again, wove through one of those angled streets in that part of town, then headed uptown.

He was going back to the house. How disappointing. I didn't know how to explain the scenic tour or trying to shake Drew, but he was only heading home. All that time and trouble, and I wasn't even going to get an adventure.

"You can't win every time, Tracy," Nuri said, when I shared my thought with him. "Believe me, this truth I've learned the hard way."

Maybe I would win this one, after all. Somewhere around East Twentieth Street, Philly abruptly jumped from his cab while it was stopped in traffic, and he headed across town on foot. Since we were a little behind and traffic was slow, I was able to continue following from the anonymous comfort of my cab. I watched as Philly scrutinized each passerby, scouring every direction but mine for anyone who might still be following him. Wherever he was headed, he didn't want company. Only when he was confident enough to stop looking over his shoulder did I let Nuri go and follow on foot.

I guessed where he was heading now — the Gramercy Park area. I was fairly comfortable with that neighborhood, though I hadn't been there in years. Dad's a member of The Players Club, which is located there. When I was little and in New York, we would take walks together through that neighborhood, and he would show me the statue of Edwin Booth. What was Philly doing there? That neighborhood was awfully rarefied for a guy whose morning newspaper had probably often doubled as his nightly blanket. Still, I saw no embarrassment in his jaunty step.

His destination proved to be a posh but tastefully understated building just off the park. A lesser man would have withered under the doorman's glare, which intimidated me from a distance. Philly seemed not to notice. Perhaps he really didn't know the gentlemen who passed through those portals didn't look like they slept in their suits.

I hid in a doorway across the street. Rats! Too far away to hear anything. I zipped across the street between some slowing cars. If Philly saw me, I was going to have to explain what I was doing there — but so was he. Inching closer until I was only a couple of feet away, I held my breath.

The doorman hung up the house phone in the recessed entry and turned to Philly. "Very well, sir. You may go up to apartment twenty-one twelve."

Okay, I had the number. Why couldn't he have used the name? Did he care that he was making extra work for me? Despite his sour expression, the doorman helped Philly into the building. I shot out of there before he could ask me why I was hanging around.

There was a little café nearby where I snagged a sidewalk table from which to plan my next move. As it was still lunchtime, they had a minimum charge; since I'd already eaten, I sat at that table nursing the most expensive cup of coffee I was ever likely to enjoy.

But the environment was congenial, even if not everyone would agree. One thing about Easterners, despite antismoking laws, lots more of them smoke than Californians. There were so many people puffing their brains out around me now — in the only part of the restaurant where it was permitted — I could actually distinguish the brands of cigarettes over the exhaust.

Back to business. How was I going to get the name of that apartment's occupant from the doorman? We don't have many doormen in Los Angeles, so I haven't had a chance to study the species. Are they as corruptible as legend holds? This one looked as solid as granite. Bet he could hit that hard, too.

Before I could decide on a strategy or finish my third cup of French roast, Philly emerged. He hadn't been inside that long, but something must have saddened him. He didn't spring off the worn heels of his old brown loafers as he had before. Philly looked a little lost, and I began to feel ashamed of my game.

He headed back toward Fifth Avenue. Having come so far, I decided to follow him back to the house, when a bland, bespectacled man in a green plaid shirt and khaki pants stopped me on the sidewalk.

"Excuse me, ma'am," he said in a Southern accent.

This tourist picked the wrong person to ask for directions. I began telling him I didn't live here, but I stopped when he placed a firm hand on my arm. He flipped his wallet open, displaying a shield.

"Detective Weaver, NYPD. Will you please come with me, ma'am? There are some questions I'd like to ask you."

What do you know? An even better adventure than the one I had in mind.

6

It could have used a coat of paint, but as holding rooms go, this one exceeded my expectations. True, the furnishings were a little basic; I remembered that scratched wooden table from my grade school library. But the plastic chairs were really pretty comfy, and the room contained enough food to survive, if I didn't mind existing on bagels and donuts. New York's finest sure know how to treat suspects. Best of all, Detective Peggy McGuire popped in occasionally to check on my comfort, or maybe just to see that I didn't make my escape. Were those guys great or what?

McGuire also dished me the dirt on Detective Weaver. She couldn't normally have been that loose-lipped, but when she learned I wrote the Tessa Graham Mystery Series, that sealed our friendship.

"Tracy, I buy your books the instant they hit the shelves. I love Tessa. She's so sharp, so witty." McGuire looked me up and down, her smile sagging somewhat. "Do you have a black belt, too?"

I brushed the leather strap circling my waist with my thumb. "Just the one I use to hold up my pants." When would they learn? If I could actually do the things Tessa does, I wouldn't have to write about them.

A comparison between me and my heroine seemed to float unspoken in the air. Unfavorable, I gathered.

Still, it broke the natural barriers between us. McGuire told me Weaver used to be a homicide investigator on the career fast track, but in the course of a case he stepped on some important toes and was transferred to another squad.

"He doesn't seem to have fallen that low." Weaver had taken me to One Police Plaza, the downtown headquarters of the NYPD. I didn't know what gig he'd landed after Homicide, but they didn't keep the dog catchers here.

McGuire's smile expressed her job satisfaction. "He was lucky to secure this berth, all right. Someone upstairs likes that good ol' boy. But Weaver's heart is still in Manhattan South Homicide. Some people just can't get enough of murder."

As someone who'd been hooked on mysteries since her first Nancy Drew book, I echoed that sentiment. Yet — I wouldn't say it there.

"It's a shame, too," McGuire went on. "Weaver's really good at what we do here."

Crunch time. I made a sympathetic sound with my tongue and affected my most casual demeanor. "Exactly . . . what is it that you . . . investigate here?"

McGuire's eyes narrowed. "Don't you know?"

She had me there. When fishing for information, it's always a mistake to show your ignorance. Too bad mine was too vast to keep hidden.

"Maybe I'd better leave that to Detective Weaver, Tracy. Do you want more coffee?" McGuire asked, before leaving me alone.

See what I mean? Loads better than *NYPD Blue* lets on. There was a shortage of reading material, but it wasn't a library. Someone had been nice enough to leave a couple of sections of yesterday's *Times*. I skimmed those, then went cover-to-cover through the flight magazine that I was still lugging around in my backpack. If I ever got sprung, I vowed to leave the magazine behind as my contribution to the room's comfort.

This was so exciting! The first time I'd been picked up by the police for questioning. Tessa knocked heads with the cops so often, it practically became her hobby. Though I had to admit I would feel less uneasy if I wasn't so damned innocent. When you have something to hide, let's face it, you can lie like a trouper — what can you do when you're not guilty, except to keep repeating that you didn't do it? Pretty lame. I wasn't nervous or anything. Not really. I just would have felt a whole lot better if I had more up my sleeve than dryer lint.

Lacking the pathetic illusion of safety in which most innocent people shroud themselves, it might be best if I didn't dwell on my situation any longer. I'd read *The Times* again, I decided. Anything was better than thinking about the shivs I would fashion from spoons and the people who would be filling my dance card should the system fail.

I caught something I missed in my first reading of the newspaper. On the front page was a photograph of the man I'd seen watching Marisa's restaurant. No wonder he looked familiar — I hadn't seen him before, just his picture. It was also not surprising I'd failed to place him. He'd weighed much more in the first photo I'd seen, while now he was lean as a hawk. Nothing ruins an appetite like an impending trial. The man studying my sister-in-law's restaurant was none other than John Anthony Briachi, the recently indicted mobster.

His driving ineptitude made sense. Godfather-types generally languish in the rear of bulletproof limos when they're trying to cut a deal. Briachi had to know his associates weren't eager to be mentioned in his upcoming testimony. What demanded such privacy it precluded the presence of a driver? And what did it have to do with The Gypsy Princess?

First, The Princess had been squeezed by Lord Hunt, now watched by Briachi. It occurred to me my sister-in-law might be in some kind of trouble. That could explain why Marisa failed to meet me. Was she making herself scarce on purpose?

Could The Princess have been the object of a struggle between Hunt and Briachi? Apart from the import business that served as a front for his illicit operations, I didn't think Briachi dabbled much in legitimate businesses. Those pesky laws were so confining. Maybe he was making a move on Hunt's arena. It wasn't hard to imagine those two sharks going at it, though I couldn't see them fighting over a cream puff.

Worst case scenario: Perhaps Briachi *already* owned The Gypsy Princess. Could he have been the silent partner Marisa alluded to the night before? Yikes! Even Charlotte would have been better.

Before I could chase those thoughts down a dark and winding road, the door opened and Detective McGuire stood aside for me to pass through. "Let's go, Tracy. The man is ready for you now."

About time. They were out of doughnuts.

∞

McGuire led me to Weaver's squad room and directed me to deposit myself on the wooden chair with the glossy varnish next to his tan metal desk. The room would have better accommodated four or five desks; the eight or so it held were a squeeze. From his spot at the window, however, Weaver's desk didn't feel quite as hemmed in. While all the tops of the scratched metal desks were lost in a sea of files and papers, they were arranged more orderly than I would have expected. None, though, were as impeccably maintained as Weaver's. How had he lined up those file tabs so precisely? The only personal objects present were a nameplate, *Detective Billy Jay Weaver*, and a photograph in an antique silver frame. Those were aligned with rigid precision as well. He'd even placed a cardboard container of coffee on a napkin.

Excessive tidiness always puts me off. Normal people are never neat; Charlotte proved that. Weaver and I glared at each other across that pristine surface, our eyes locked in a bitter struggle that acknowledged the old adage: He who speaks first loses. I didn't have a clue what there was to win, but whatever it was, it was mine. He broke first — but he managed to turn his loss into a victory.

"I talked to someone in the Los Angeles Police Department about you, Ms. Eaton. You have quite a reputation out there."

"I do?" Be still my heart — he was confusing me with someone else. Creating enough havoc to be known by the police was my life's goal.

"Did you really chain yourself to a judge's car because they wouldn't give you a jury trial for a traffic ticket?" Weaver asked with almost utter disbelief.

"Oh — that." A big nothing. The press discovered it — well, my phone calls helped — and they dropped the citation. Never even got cuffed. "There's no such thing as a small injustice," I added with dignity.

The bastard giggled. I was a tough adversary engaged in a brutal contest of wills, and he made me feel like I slipped on a banana.

"You had to be there," I said.

"I guess that's so, ma'am."

Ma'am? He was so much the Southern gentlemen, he should have been wearing a white suit and selling chicken instead of busting relatively innocent tourists.

"What did you do?" I asked. "Take a wrong turn at Biloxi?"

"You mean — why am I here in New York? Well, Leila — that's my wife — Leila took it in her head to be a model. And you know how the song goes, whatever Leila wants, Leila gets."

Wasn't that *Lola*?

"I've never been able to deny anything to that girl. But Leila and me, we 'bout had enough of this place. One of these days, I reckon we'll be heading home."

The wannabes never stopped pursuing the bright lights. I'd seen them all my life, seen what happened to most of them. I sincerely hoped the Big Apple was not too hard on little Leila from Arkansas. The photograph on Weaver's desk of the skinny, pale blonde *sans* makeup convinced me she didn't have a prayer.

Silence returned. To show how little it troubled him, Weaver removed his thick glasses for an unnecessary cleaning. Bad move.

You shouldn't have done that, Billy Jay, I thought. You should have just kept being the poor schmuck from Dixie. True, I never bought the good ol' boy act, but I didn't know where it ended. It was a mistake to take those glasses off and let me see that his were the eyes of a man who had never been any kind of a fool.

Something in my face must have told him he'd goofed. Quickly, he became very businesslike. "Look, Ms. Eaton, we both have better things to do. Why don't you just tell me what you were doing when I stopped you."

Why was I fighting him? Maybe I'd simply stumbled onto their stakeout. Asking stuff like that was his job.

"It's a little hard to explain. Perhaps I should give you some background. You see, I'm a mystery writer. I'm the author of the Tessa Graham Mystery Series."

I paused expectantly.

He cleared his throat. "Have you written anything else I might recognize?"

Police brutality yet! This guy played hardball.

I did a verbal one-eighty. "Why should I tell you what I was doing?"

"Maybe I stated the question wrong, ma'am. I know what you were doing. Hundreds of people know what you were doing, and if New Yorkers weren't so blasé, they all would have gawked. I had you spotted the instant you started following him."

"Impossible," I said.

"Sidling along building fronts, popping into doorways. I never saw anything so — "

"All right!" I snapped. As soon as I stopped thinking about his assault on my detective prowess, I started making connections. "You were following him, too!"

Weaver's silence confirmed it.

"You were! That's crazy." This was Drew's uncle we were talking about, even if he didn't fit the mold. "Believe me, Detective Weaver, you have the wrong man. You can't imagine how wrong. What is it you think he's done?"

Weaver took a slow sip of coffee. "I don't remember saying I thought he did anything."

"Yeah, right. NYPD detectives have so little to do, they drag innocent people in just for looking at other innocent people."

"Let's just say I'm interested in anybody interested in Philly Chase," Weaver said.

"That's so nuts. Wait a sec — What did you say?"

"I said I'm — "

"The name, the name," I snapped.

"Philly Chase, of course." Weaver frowned, confused.

I slapped my hand against my thigh. "There you have it. This has all been a huge misunderstanding. We're not talking about the same man."

"Well now, ma'am, you might know him by one of his other names, but I assure you Philly Chase is the one on the birth certificate."

"You have this all wrong, Detective. Charlotte — that's my mother-in-law — Charlotte's maiden name is Cord, and she's Philly's sister." No doubt there. Charlotte was so proud of her family name, she gave it as a middle name to both of her sons. Only Marisa Irina escaped that fate — which was funny when you thought about it, but this didn't seem to be the time to do that. "This Mr. Chase can't be Charlotte's brother."

"I don't know anything about Philly's mama and what she might have done, but I do know you and I were watching the same man. What are the odds there were two men named Phillip on the same block — grown men now, mind you — calling themselves Philly?" He snorted derisively.

"Almost as long as two calling themselves Billy Jay, I'd say." I stared pointedly at that idiotic name plate.

"Low blow, ma'am." But a smile gleamed in his deep blue eyes.

"I'm stunned," I admitted more candidly than usual, proving the truth of my statement.

Weaver rose. "I am sorry about that. Now, Ms. Eaton, I think we got to the bottom of this business, and you best be on your way before someone starts worrying about you. I surely do appreciate your help."

He was tossing me out; he'd discovered there wasn't anything worth wringing out of me. I didn't need a second invitation to leave. I stood up and started walking toward the exit, but stopped after only a couple of steps and faced him.

"Detective, you still haven't told me what you suspect Philly of doing."

"No, I haven't."

"Won't you at least tell me what division of the police department this is?"

He hesitated, then shrugged. "What we have here is the Special Frauds Squad."

7

The Special Frauds Squad? Was Weaver trying to say Philly was some hotshot con man? How could he possibly think that about Drew's uncle? Why was Philly's name different from his sister's? And what was that bit about him using different names?

WHAT THE HELL WAS GOING ON? I wondered for the twelve zillionth time.

I saw Nuri's cab idling in a loading zone when I left Weaver's office, which both surprised and moved me.

"How did you know where I'd be?" I asked him.

"I drove back through that neighborhood after my next fare, and I saw the police taking you away, Tracy. So I waited here. My shift is over, but I thought you might need a ride home."

That wonderful man. Was I ever grateful. The cabs were thinning out and a rush-hour subway was not the best place for serious thinking. My mind overflowed with questions. I *had* to get to the bottom of this. I couldn't stand not knowing. The leverage it would give me over Charlotte would be too good to pass up, even if I never used it.

It must have taken an eternity to reach the Eaton home in that heavy traffic, but I scarcely noticed. I was still toying with ways to get the scoop on Philly without alerting the family to my suspicions when Drew and his mother tackled me at the front door, demanding to know where Marisa was.

I didn't know then that the questions Philly raised would soon pale in significance. Neither did I imagine that the fun and games had already ended — and a nightmare none of us would ever forget was just beginning.

I did have some inkling, however, that my world had already taken a detour through *The Twilight Zone*. From the instant I walked through the door, the situation became progressively stranger. Drew denied that he had been following his uncle. Why would he lie about that? It was such a sensible move, it should have been right up his alley. Philly needed a keeper. He also told that ridiculous lie about not leaving the house, when I knew I'd seen him. How could he hope to put that one over?

Then I learned that Marisa was still missing, and while I refused to admit it, worry began to build a boulder of regrets in the pit of my stomach. Why didn't I go straight to her apartment? She could have been hurt. Why didn't I chase Drew and enlist his help in finding her, instead of tailing Philly?

When the doorbell rang, I leapt at the chance to answer it. I didn't trust myself to be left alone with my liar husband — he was too well-insured. I also needed to see Marisa, to prove to myself that she was really all right, that my silly games hadn't endangered her life. But when the banging on the door began, I froze, sensing the fear I felt wasn't going to go away anytime soon.

"Can't one of you answer that? Or do I have to do everything?" Charlotte-the-martyr called from the den.

Drew came up behind me. "Tracy?"

"Right."

I grasped the knob and turned it, but before I'd pulled the door more than a few inches, Tony pushed it open and rushed past me. Drew and I ran to the living room behind him. When we reached him, he was twisting his head from side-to-side, searching for something that clearly wasn't there.

"Is-a she here? Marisa, she came here?" Tony demanded in that garbled accent.

"Isn't she at the restaurant?" My throat tightened.

"She no been there all-a day."

"She's not here, Tony," Drew said. "We've been looking for her ourselves."

"Marisa?" Charlotte asked when she joined us. "*Everyone* has been looking for her. At least a dozen people have called for her here."

"Then — it's-a no joke," Tony cried.

"What isn't?" Drew asked.

Tony opened his mouth, but nothing came out. He pinched his eyes closed.

"Tony, what's wrong?" I shouted.

"It's Marisa. A woman — she called today. *Dio mio*. It cannot be true!"

"Tony, you're scaring us," I said. "What happened?"

"Marisa's kidnapped!"

"No!" Charlotte said in a hoarse whisper.

Tony collapsed into a chair and looked up at us with a grimace of long-borne pain and bitterness.

8

"Kidnapped!" Charlotte said with a whimper. She closed her eyes, but not before one sad little tear escaped down her cheek. "It can't be true."

The horror in her voice spoke for all of us. Though it had been well over an hour since Tony made his announcement, we were still too stunned to take it in.

"No way. Got to be a joke." Corbett knocked back a short neat bourbon in a crystal rocks glass. "Some sickos just get off on cruelty. They don't actually do what they threaten. They don't," he repeated in an obvious attempt to convince himself.

"Sometimes, son, they're only uncaring and avaricious, but they do precisely what they threaten," Taylor said kindly. He yanked his tie off and loosened the top button of his shirt with a heavy sigh. "Besides, if it is a joke, it's being perpetrated by someone who knows Marisa's been incommunicado today."

"And why hasn't she called anyone if she can?" Charlotte demanded. She punctuated her remarks by waving the pad and pen she clutched. She had taken them from the burl desk along the wall, from which she ran her household, though she hadn't used them for anything but extensions of her nervous hands. "If she wasn't injured or . . . anything, can you imagine your sister not honoring her commitments?" She pointed emphatically at Corbett with the pen. "Give me one good reason."

My mind had spit out a few good reasons why Marisa had failed to show up while I'd waited for Weaver, though I had to admit the kidnapping scenario fit better than most. Unfortunately, I would rather have believed Marisa was just laying low until whatever jam she'd gotten into was over. We could have fixed that.

"Tony, you're sure the person who called was a woman?" Philly asked.

Those odd little tufts of hair that stuck out from his head the night before had multiplied. Now he looked like the world's oldest punk. Obviously, he'd been running his hands through his coarse hair. Drew had had enough presence of mind to summon his father and brother from their offices, and they had joined us where we huddled together in the den. No one had given a thought to Philly, but he toddled in about ten minutes later and quickly became as unglued as everyone else.

"No. Not sure. Voice was — how you say? — low," Tony said.

"That's how you say it, Tony," I muttered.

My remark might have sounded flippant, but I had a reason for it. Drew could have given me the benefit of the doubt before shooting me that ugly look.

"Traffic sounds in background," Tony said, less the feeble immigrant now. "She — or he — spoke soft. I think it was a woman." Tony showed his confusion with a helpless lift of his shoulders.

"Old? Young?" Philly slipped from his spot on the sofa to perch on the edge of the coffee table, leaning toward Tony. "Educated?"

"Young . . . I believe." Tony sagged back into the blue chair I'd found so cozy the night before; judging by his gloomy frown, he didn't consider it nearly so inviting.

Philly rested his elbows on his knees for support and leaned closer still. "American? European?"

"Don't know!" Tony leaped to his feet and rushed blindly toward the far wall. The fingers of his right hand curled into a fist. His forearm muscles grew so tight, I feared he might put his fist through the wall. Tony caught himself and just gave the patterned wallpaper above the walnut wainscoting a slow, absent tap.

"Come on, boy," Philly snapped. "You must remember something more."

The scorched smell of something burning irritated my nostrils. Nobody else seemed to notice. I traced the smell to the kitchen, where I found a crusty roast in the oven and a few pots that had boiled over on the stove. I considered checking to see what I could salvage; instead, I just switched off the power to everything and left it where it was.

When I returned to the den, I remained in the doorway watching the others. It amazed me that Taylor and Charlotte could pace in the same space without colliding. Time and again, they unconsciously slid past each other without seeming to notice. Corbett batted his empty glass back and forth between his hands, sliding it nosily across the coffee table. Tony sat on the floor leaning into the sofa like that was all that held him up. I paused a moment to pick up the conversational thread, but they seemed to have slipped into a troubled silence.

Philly slouched in the cushy blue chair now, his chin pressed to his chest. While fear for my sister-in-law consumed me, my mind engaged in a little peripheral speculation about the mysterious Mr. Chase. I certainly saw him in a new light. There was unexpected depth there, though it might simply have been a cesspool.

Good ol' Uncle Philly did seem every bit as crushed as Charlotte and Taylor — even more agitated — but he was a less contained person. In contrast to all of them, Tony looked positively destroyed.

Philly absently pulled his stained old Meerschaum pipe and a battered packet of Flying Dutchman from his coat pocket. He leaned over the coffee table to fill the pipe, but his hands shook. He sprinkled tobacco on the surface. Charlotte started to object, but Drew silently took his mother's wrist and shook his head. She seemed to agree to let it go with an irritated flick of her shoulders.

Drew caught my eye and indicated, with a toss of his head, the rosewood cabinet in the corner. I wasn't sure what he wanted until I opened the cabinet door and saw a glass ashtray from an Atlantic City casino. When I placed it before Philly, a ghost of his old smile flickered, and he told me he left that ashtray there years ago. And I was hoping Charlotte had stolen it.

Despite my doubts about him, I couldn't stand to see Philly so funny-looking. I reached out and smoothed down his ruffled hair with my fingertips. He rewarded me with another smile before turning back to his pipe. Philly beat the tobacco into the bowl with a vicious tapping of his pipe tool. He tore a match from a well-used matchbook with a bright blue martini glass on the cover, and he lit the pipe.

Breathing in the sweet smell of the burning tobacco, I nearly begged him for a puff. I wasn't doing that well myself. I normally consider self-flagellation to be a counterproductive act, but I had to struggle not to engage in it now. While Marisa feared for her life, I had been making a perfect ass of myself before an audience of police officers.

It occurred to me to question my assumption about the timing of today's events. How did I know where Marisa was when I became an ass? When had she been abducted? The clearer we could be on that, the better Marisa's chances were. I leaned across Drew, who was seated on the arm of the grey lounge chair, and snatched up the pad and pen his mother had discarded on the coffee table.

"Tony," I asked, flicking the pen against the surface of the pad, "when did you last see Marisa?"

"This morning. Early," Tony said.

"Tracy, is that important now?" Drew asked.

While Drew fixed me in his angry stare, Corbett just looked at me through the empty glass he held before his eyes. If he was hinting he wanted a refill, I had better things to do. What was it with these lawyers? Were they *all* hopeless airheads? Surely Drew appreciated the importance of establishing Marisa's day. I ignored both of them and nodded for Tony to continue.

"I decide I should-a go to restaurant early. Marisa, she no going to be there, and I have more to do." Tony's English was still atrocious, but at least he enunciated now. "I no expect her to get up early like me. I write her a note. I no think I will see her, but she gets up anyway. She say she has much to do before she meets you. Calls, errands, maybe early aerobics class. She is-a still in apartment when I go."

His eyes glazed over as he drifted off into thought, remembering perhaps the last thing he said to her and how it might have differed — if he had known it could actually have been the last thing.

I found myself thinking about the beginning of my own day when I remembered something significant. Before I could get to it, Philly diverted things again.

"Tony, go back to the woman on the phone. You said you thought she might have been young." Puff, puff. "What made you think that?" Puff, puff, puff.

He sure kept hitting on that, and I didn't see the loose, scattered Philly Chase as an obsessive.

Taylor began to pace again. He held his tie folded in his clenched hand and unconsciously swung it at pieces of furniture. "It's doubtful the woman on the phone was all that important, Philly. She's probably just the girlfriend of one of the kidnappers or someone hired to make the call. I might be an old chauvinist, but I think you expect a kidnapper to be a man. Perhaps they've used her to confuse us."

"Not necessarily, Taylor." Perching next to Drew, I described my near-miss with the van outside the bridal shop, and the gender of its driver. "If Marisa had gone for her fitting as planned, she might have been plucked off the sidewalk there."

"Would you know her — if you saw her again, Tracy?" Corbett asked.

I closed my eyes and tried to bring up the image. It was ironic that she'd generated that fleeting sense of familiarity in me this morning; now there was no longer even a shadowy image in the blank space I jokingly called my mind.

"No . . . well, maybe in the right context — " I shrugged.

"It's unlikely that she was anything other than someone late with a delivery," Taylor said. "Marisa could have been picked up anywhere. We have no reason to believe it happened there."

"I'm not making myself clear, Taylor. I know this sounds paranoid, but I'd swear that woman was *trying* to run me down. Damn near did, too. If my reflexes were an instant slower, I'd be in the morgue now."

Taylor stopped before me. "Why, Tracy? Don't kidnappers like to keep the family alive so someone can pay them off? And how did this person know you were part of the family? If they've been watching us for a while, as they undoubtedly have, they wouldn't have seen you and Drew. You don't live around here."

I sighed and shook my head. Taylor's questions were good ones, and I had no answers.

My father-in-law gave my hand a squeeze. "Thanks for trying, sweetheart, but you're just not accustomed to dodging our aggressive New York drivers."

That was the obvious explanation, wasn't it? But why couldn't I shake the feeling that it wasn't a matter of the driver simply not caring *whether* she hit me, but of *trying* to? If the rest of the family had experienced no close calls, why would I have been singled out?

Drew draped his arm around my shoulders. "My father's right, Tracy. We're not used to the way they treat pedestrians here. I grew up in New York, and I still had to step lively a few times today."

Really? I thought he hadn't left the house all day. Or so he had claimed. I wiggled out from under his arm.

"My poor baby," Charlotte said, absently giving voice to her pain. "*Our* baby," she amended.

She rose from the sofa and moved to the window. On the way, her hand paused a moment on her brother's shoulder. The first gesture of affection I'd seen between them. But a tragedy involving a loved one often brings people closer. Though she had to notice Philly scattered more ash than Mount St. Helens, Charlotte didn't complain.

"It's getting cold out," Charlotte said in a small voice. Her hands gripped the drapery cords at the front window, but she refrained from closing the drapes. Did she feel she'd be closing her daughter out along with the evening if she pulled them shut?

"Tony, you said there was something odd about the ransom," Drew remembered now.

"Good God — the ransom!" Taylor said. "I forgot all about it."

He and Charlotte exchanged a long look. They were moderately wealthy people, but I could see they worried they wouldn't be able to meet it. Corbett went to the bar and grabbed the bourbon bottle. His hands shook.

"How much?" Charlotte asked.

"Ransom is-a not money. We will even make-a some money," Tony explained wearily.

Caught pouring himself a drink, Corbett stopped mid-pour. "How's that again, buddy?"

"Must-a sell the restaurant," Tony said.

"To raise the money to meet the kidnapper's demand, you mean?" Charlotte asked. "That isn't necessary, Tony dear. Taylor and I will pay the ransom."

"You no understand, Charlotte. Selling The Gypsy Princess — that *is* the ransom."

"I don't get it. The kidnapper wants you to sell the restaurant?" Drew asked.

"Not wants — insists."

Drew frowned. "What if you can't find a buyer?"

"It has-a been arranged. That is part of the ransom." The way Tony ran his hands through his soft brown hair made him look like he was ready to explode from frustration.

Corbett took a gulp and immediately replaced it. "Come again, Tony?"

"For Marisa to return alive, we must-a sell restaurant to a particular buyer," Tony explained haltingly.

"Who?" Taylor demanded.

"Lord Hunt."

9

"*He* must-a be the one behind it," Tony said with passionate intensity, as he wore a path in the rug.

I wondered about his emphasis. He almost sounded as if he were fingering one suspected kidnapper over another, when I didn't know an assortment existed.

"You mean — Hunt?" I asked from the desk.

Tony stopped and faced me. "Hunt always want The Gypsy Princess. And he is a man who gets what he wants."

Taylor sat heavily on the sofa between Charlotte and Drew. He had rolled up his sleeves — a first, I never knew he had forearms. But his voice retained the practiced assurance he brought to the courtroom. "Hunt does play a little close to the edge, but he's always been careful."

"It must-a be Hunt," Tony insisted, pounding his fist against a chair.

Drew jumped to his feet. "Tony, get real. No one paints a bull's-eye on himself."

"Not someone as sharp as Hunt," Taylor insisted.

"Maybe that what he want us to think," Tony suggested. "Who else gains?"

Drew went to the bar. He opened the little refrigerator hidden in the base behind a wooden cabinet door and took a jar of green olives from it. He tossed a few into his hand, as he reasoned slowly. "Perhaps someone who knows Hunt has tried to buy The Princess and has set this thing up to frame him. There are all kinds of gains." Drew threw a cautious glance his mother's way before munching on the olives.

"That's farfetched, Drew, even for the world of corporate intrigue," Corbett insisted. "I thought Tracy was the fiction writer."

"And this whole thing isn't farfetched?" Drew's face reddened in anger. "Have you ever heard of such a crazy ransom?"

The brothers descended into bickering, which their mother brought to a halt by clapping her hands. I didn't pay much attention to them. This runaway speculation had started to seem not only pointless but perplexing. True, when people hurt, sometimes it helps to talk things through. But they could do that once the wheels of justice were set in motion.

"Talking about it isn't getting us anywhere," I said. "The police will find out who is behind it." I moved over to the desk and lifted the receiver on the phone.

"No!" they all shouted simultaneously.

"No police!" Tony said for the entire group.

I hung up but kept my hand on the phone. "Look, I can't believe these words are coming from my mouth, either. But we have to call the police. We're not equipped to handle this."

Tony rushed at me. "The woman who call, she say-a no police!"

"They always say that, and the family of the victim calls them anyway. They're our only hope," I argued as forcefully as I could.

Philly took my hand from the phone and held it. "Bad move, kiddo."

"Taylor . . . ?" Charlotte asked in a voice that spoke volumes, none of which were written in a language I understood.

Taylor moved to the desk and leaned on it, as he might against the jury box railing. "I think calling in the police would be the wrong move at this juncture."

"Agreed," Corbett said.

"Ditto," my husband concurred.

They had surrounded me! If they had slapped me in the face, their intentions could not have been clearer.

Charlotte smoothed out the wrinkles in her black linen dress. "Tracy dear, if you go into the kitchen, you'll find a tray of cheese and crackers on the counter. Your husband needs something to eat."

Now they were kicking me out!

From the kitchen, I could hear the buzz of voices, but not what they were saying. The talking stopped when I returned with the cheese platter, which I dropped heavily onto the coffee table. If the stakes weren't so damned high, I might have laughed at the irony of it all. I was supposed to be the freewheeling one in this bunch. But I was the only one in support of the conventional approach. For once, I couldn't understand how anyone could do anything else.

I grabbed a bottle of wine from the rack at the top of the bar and a corkscrew from the drawer. "If you're not calling the police, what *do* you intend to *do*?" To my ears, my voice sounded almost harsh and demanding; well, maybe it was. They were pissing me off.

Taylor tapped his hands together in a gesture of finality. "Only one thing to do, Tracy. We'll pay the ransom."

I almost dropped the wine. "Sell the restaurant? Tony, is that what you want?"

He shrugged. "No choice."

"But to sell Marisa's beloved restaurant? When she comes back, she won't have anything!"

"They can always start another restaurant," Charlotte snapped. "This time we'll give them the money."

Like that would have made a difference.

"You said the co-op had to remain strong or none of you would survive." I handed the bottle to Corbett; that was his domain.

Corbett grabbed the bottle from my hand. "Are you suggesting the co-op is more important than Marisa's life?" he demanded in outrage.

The cold front was really moving in now, ready to dump a load of snow on me. I felt as if my mere presence had become offensive to one and all.

"Then we're all agreed," Drew concluded. "Corbett, draw up the papers. Tony will sign them."

"Uh . . . I think we're forgetting something." Corbett stopped peeling the foil from the wine bottle. "Uncle Philly . . . ?"

A tiny crack developed in their wall of togetherness. As the attorney for The Gypsy Princess and the co-op, Corbett was obviously privy to some information the others lacked. That it concerned Philly didn't surprise me in the least. The eyes of his *compañeros* all honed in on Corbett, while I turned to Philly. And I actually caught him plotting something, sitting there on a foot stool near his sister's side, untidy as ever — but no longer out of place. Sure, his bland expression beamed with innocence, but he couldn't hide the conniving look in his eyes as the little wheels of his mind searched for a way to slip their gears.

Whoa! Was that how I looked sometimes? Can people really tell? Scary thought.

"I guess we'd better tell you. It's a little late for secrets," Corbett said. "Philly is the third owner of The Gypsy Princess."

Wide-eyed, Charlotte asked, "Phillip, is this true?"

Philly's nodding reminded me of one of those dogs with the bobbing heads you see in the hat racks of cars. Philly was dancing as fast as he could, all right.

Charlotte's angry blue eyes found Tony. "Tony, I don't understand this. You rejected our offer of help, but you allowed this — this — "

"Don't have a cow, Charlotte. The kids were just doing me a favor." Philly refilled his pipe. "I — kinda — came into some money, and Marisa thought investing in the restaurant would be a way to keep me from blowing it. You know, so I could save it for my retirement."

"Retirement!" Charlotte snorted.

"My dear sister," Philly said, "a lady doesn't speak with her nose." The old fox was quoting her.

From the sofa, Charlotte jumped to her feet. "How would you know? Have you ever met any? I remember —"

Taylor stepped between them. "Charlotte! Philly! This isn't getting us anywhere. There isn't any problem. Char-

lotte, we *know* Philly will do whatever he can to bring
Marisa back."

"Of course I will." There was no mistaking the passion in Philly's response.

"There," Taylor said.

"There's just one problem, Taylor," Philly added.

"Yes?" Taylor leaned forward, waiting and tense.

"I don't own my share anymore. I sold it." Lighting
his pipe now claimed all of Philly's attention.

His sister couldn't seem to resist taunting him. "I
thought you were saving it for your retirement."

Philly shrugged.

"Who bought your share, Philly?" Drew sounded like
he was coaxing something from a difficult child.

"A guy I know. He's a good guy. He'll be glad to sell
it back."

"Then it's no problem." Drew looked at each of his
parents, as if to reassure them.

"*If* we can find him," Philly added.

"Where did you see him last?" Drew's control was
growing threadbare.

"Orly Airport in Paris just before I flew here," Philly
said.

Charlotte groaned. "*Paris?*"

"Where was he going?" Taylor cried in exasperation.

Philly scratched his head. "He didn't say."

10

Philly's announcement that he no longer owned his share in The Gypsy Princess pretty much nuked the family's hope. Though they rallied well. And when the Eatons mobilized, their determination could be formidable, even if not well directed.

Immediately, Corbett flew to Paris to be on hand to carry out the legal matters when the third owner of The Princess was found. *If* he was. Charlotte loaned me her new silver Volvo to drive him to the airport. She couldn't have warned me more than a hundred times not to bring it back dented, but she was distracted.

Naturally, the flight was fully booked at this date, but by appealing to everyone in the check-in line, we managed to find one person willing to relinquish her vacation-of-a-lifetime ticket. Don't ask what he paid for it; she can now take the vacation of everyone's life.

Drew moved into an empty room in his father's office to carry out his part of the search over the telephone. But first, of course, they questioned Philly.

Taylor started it off. "What's this man's name, Philly?"

"Man?" Philly asked.

Now they moved in to encircle him where he sat.

"The man who bought your share of the restaurant, silly," Charlotte added.

Philly fiddled with his pipe. "Oh, that man."

"Yes, that man!" Taylor snapped. "What is his name?"

"Al," Philly said.

Drew took over for his frustrated father. "Does Al have a last name?"

"Dumont. It's Al Dumont."

"A Frenchman?" Charlotte asked.

"Don't know. Could be. When Al and I get together, we always speak — Spanish. *Hablas español?*"

"*Sí*," Drew said.

"Oh."

I would have said I considered him suspiciously vague, only understatement wasn't my style. The others were as happy with his offerings as new parents whose baby has just learned to drool. I understood they were simply postponing their skepticism, but when those questions returned, they were going to be devastated. They were also gambling with Marisa's life.

Now me, I was a different breed of cat. Sure, I'd engaged in some denial of my own, but the time for that luxury had passed. And I did not believe in giving in to extortion. If I had my way, the best of New York's finest or the FBI would be scouring this town for the bastard who abducted Marisa. But that was not in the cards the Eatons dealt.

Drawing the only possible conclusion: If justice was going to prevail, it would obviously need my help.

⚭

I began my investigation at the airport. Once we secured the ticket, Corbett insisted that I leave, rather than walking him to the gate. I wished him good luck and departed with a cheery wave. But I crept back and watched till I saw him board.

I hated doubting Drew's brother. But he was drinking much too much, and he faced what threatened to be an expensive divorce. He'd also had more contact with Hunt than anyone else. Sure, he loved Marisa, but he'd never been as close to his sister and brother as Drew and Marisa were to each other. People can rationalize almost anything. Trust me, I had real firsthand knowledge of that.

Just to be sure, I would wangle the number where Corbett was staying from Drew and try it once or twice myself. After all, planes crossed the Atlantic the other way, too.

I dropped the car off at Charlotte's garage and returned to the townhouse. I wanted to change into jeans and tennies, and to stuff my backpack with the equipment to face every eventuality that might arise. I didn't expect to hit my first roadblock so soon.

Drew was waiting for me at the house upon my return. I had assumed he'd gone to the office with his father, but he had the cockeyed idea that I would tag along with him and try to trace The Princess's other owner, since he didn't seem to have much faith in Al Dumont.

While I inched backward through the foyer, he continued his approach.

"It's right up your alley, Tracy. After years of writing

about an amateur detective, I thought sure you'd know how to find the buyer through financial transactions."

I didn't know the first thing about financial traces, and he knew it. I suspected — no, I was certain, he had been delegated to keep an eye on me. "Gee, I wish I could, but — what are the odds? I ran into my editor at the airport. Now she insists on meeting with me. Why, I don't know. Anyway, I'm off to — "

Drew's eyes narrowed to suspicious slits. "I thought Carolyn was on vacation. Didn't you tell me she went to Naples for three weeks?"

Jeez, I needed to start using a crib sheet. "Naples, *Florida*." Thank you, Mrs. Howard, for fourth grade geography. "For three *days*. She's back."

Charlotte came up behind Drew and listened with interest.

"The only way I can get out of it would be to tell her about Marisa." I looked to Charlotte. "I know you don't want me to do that."

Charlotte brushed a speck of dust from the small Japanese table in the foyer. "Tracy dear, isn't it time you forgot all this writing nonsense and found some worthwhile cause that would appreciate the volunteer efforts of a young wife in your position?"

I gasped speechlessly. Something in my brain combusted, and I took a step forward.

Drew rushed between us. "Trace, you better get going. You know how Carolyn hates to be kept waiting."

I didn't grin — until I was safely on the other side of the front door. I know them pretty well, too.

Next stop: I returned to the scene of the crime. Not mine — Philly's. Not his, either, for all I knew. But I was back at the building he visited the day before. I didn't really think his mystery friend had anything to do with Marisa's kidnapping — that would have been too easy — but Philly went to great lengths to hide his visit there. Besides, the logical starting point of any investigation is the person who acts the most guilty. If that description didn't fit Philly, the skies rained gold.

Not that I believed him to be directly involved in this crime. I saw genuine love between Philly and his sister's children, especially Marisa. But events tend to get away from people like Philly. If nothing else, that funny little man raised too many questions.

I took refuge once again on the smoky café patio while I staked out the building. This time I didn't make do with overpriced coffee; I came prepared with a newspaper and hunger.

My chicken-and-mushroom crepes were great, but I just couldn't keep my mind off the events of the night before. I'd never exactly been an insider in the Eaton family, but I'd gradually been accepted. I didn't know a cold shoulder could pack such a wallop. With both families opposed to our marriage at the start, Drew and I were united against everyone. Who knew that over time old bonds would prove the stronger? I searched through my backpack for a packet of tissues and blew my nose. Damned smoke was burning my eyes. No way was I crying. I swear.

If I looked at the situation objectively, I could discount

some of the Eatons' treatment of me. Desperate people do desperate things. Unfortunately, I couldn't write it all off to their concern for Marisa. I'd never noticed before that I was related to a pack of liars. Well, never on Drew's side. Those people were hiding something. Were they all hiding the same thing? Could there be that many guilty secrets?

Taking a fortifying whiff of the smoky air, I returned to watching the building. I wanted to catch its flow, assess the comings and goings of its residents, gauge how bribery-friendly the doorman was. Trouble was, the place was dead. No comings, no goings, and the doorman sat in the lobby reading the paper.

Sensible man; I did the same.

Briachi made the news again. In carefully worded quotes, his attorney hinted at their desire to cut a deal. I could build a case for Briachi's involvement purely on the basis of his character. Somehow, it didn't smell right to me.

While I believed in the principle of innocent until proven guilty, I was equally sure Briachi did everything of which he stood accused. And then some. If ever there was a time when he would want to keep a low profile, it had to be now while the legal and media spotlights were directed at him. But this was the man who risked his skin — staking out The Gypsy Princess.

Maybe Briachi was the third owner of The Princess. I hadn't bought Philly's story about selling his share to the first name that popped into his head, but it might not have been a total lie. Was it such a stretch to imagine Philly involved with the mob? I would have pegged Philly as more

of a small-time con artist, but Weaver's interest in him ne-
gated that. Weaver's squad trolled for bigger fish. Besides,
I remembered the way Philly handled that doorman. A lack
of confidence wasn't his problem.

I could accept that sooner than believe Marisa or Tony
might have been dumb enough to give a mobster a share.
Besides, what chance would they have had to meet a man
like Briachi?

Some movement at the front of the building caught
my eye. Just a blue-haired helmet-head waiting for her limo.
Nothing important, I thought, and returned my attention
to the newspaper. I quickly glanced back up; it occurred to
me that perhaps I *had* seen something useful. I watched —
until another resident emerged. No dice; this guy took a
cab. The third tenant was better for my purposes. Again, a
parking attendant brought the car to the entrance. The vehicles for the residents of this building were all coming
from somewhere around the corner.

I paid my check and hit the streets. I struggled to control my excitement. My first case! I'd been writing about
the exploits of an amateur sleuth for so long, I knew it all.
What could go wrong?

I roamed around the block like I was lost or hunting
for an address. Then there it was; I found the entrance to
the garage, where I stationed myself. Not as simple as it
sounded. People in expensive neighborhoods frown on loi-
terers. Too bad I hadn't bought a pack of cigarettes, purely
as a prop. With a little creative stretching, you can kill five
minutes finding and lighting a cigarette. Twice that in the
wind. Luckily, I still had shoelaces. By the time I tied the
second one, a car was just pulling out. I slipped through

the electric gates, then sidled up alongside the first car I happened upon to case the joint.

If I hadn't known how pricey the neighborhood was, the vehicles housed in that garage would have convinced me. Nothing but limousines, Mercedes, and Rolls Royces, with the odd BMW thrown in just to be democratic. Of course, there were too many people there for my purposes. Valet attendants, chauffeurs, mechanics, even the occasional resident; they might've been having a convention. A lower profile than comes natural for me was clearly required.

I sank to my knees. What great foresight I'd shown when I changed into jeans and sneakers — I was ready for anything. If I'd owned one of those apartments, the poor lighting and minuscule parking spaces would have outraged me. Someone should tell them forty-watt bulbs don't cut it in a dungeon. Not to worry, I always carried a small flashlight. I thrust my hand into my backpack. Luckily, a sudden collective whoop from a cluster of men watching a televised football game in the far corner covered the sounds of my rummaging. I grasped something that felt like a chubby ballpoint.

That was it, all right, just as I remembered: A slim, green penlight with the words, *Willie's Foreign Car Repair*, printed along the side. We'd given ol' Willie a shot at our cars several years ago. If memory served, he wasn't much of a mechanic, but his promotional giveaways were first-rate. I clicked it on. Too bad Willie hadn't thought to come by and change the batteries sometime in the last few years.

Okay, that was lesson one for the new detective.

Not a tragedy. I just had to stick my head under the cars to read the apartment numbers painted in the spaces.

I'd crawled halfway along one row before I grasped the really bad news. The stall assignments were in random order! What kind of idiot would set up a garage that way?

I crawled through row after row. I'm a pretty optimistic person, as a rule, until something impinges on my minimum comfort level — something I'd now left way behind. The knees of my jeans, as well as my body, were never going to be the same again. Permanent dimples had been pressed into the heels of my hands, and I'd scraped the side of my face trying to look under a low-slung sports car. Hell, I was probably leaving a trail of blood, even if it was too dark to see it. There was also too much foot traffic. Again and again, an attendant would dash past, and I'd have to flatten myself to the floor. Good thing I was almost ethereal.

I'm generally determined, too. If I felt crabby, it was only because I feared I'd already blown it. I had thrown myself in there armed with nothing more than the number of the apartment Philly visited. When I found the parking stall that corresponded to it, I was certain I would learn something about its occupant. But what if I didn't? What if the stall was empty when I finally found it, or what if it had been one of those I couldn't read too well and had already passed? What if the car door was locked and I couldn't get at the registration? The kidnapper wasn't going to wait forever. If this proved to be a hopeless mistake, how would I recover the time?

No, it was too soon to quit. I crawled faster, concentrating so hard on the numbers that I forgot to listen for sounds — until my nose slammed into a pair of wing tips. Now, in my experience, shoes don't enter garages unaccompanied by persons. Twisting my neck around, I saw attached to these shoes a well-dressed elderly man who didn't look like he appreciated the fun in finding strange women stuck under his car.

"Urg," was my pathetic response. Jeez, was that the best I could do? I was going to have to lie; well, I needed the practice.

Amazingly, that feeble reaction worked. "You're one of Dave's women, aren't you?" A strange look stole over the man's face. My guess was he'd made that odd expression by mixing a small amount of wishing he were Dave with a whole bunch of relief that he was not.

I smiled vaguely, unsure of what reaction one of Dave's women would have. Would the members of a harem want to be reminded of the rest of the group? Either my reaction satisfied him, or he just wanted to get away.

"Good luck," he said, climbing into his car.

Sure. I fell back on my butt, wondering how I could get out of this mess. Then I noticed something. The truth was, I'd been having trouble reading some of the stall numbers in that low light. Once that man backed out, the stalls to each side and the front of it were better lit. And guess what? Yeah, one of those stalls was for apartment number twenty-one twelve!

Frankly, I'd rather be lucky than good. Lucky? I'd just hit the mother lode. I hardly knew anyone in New York. Thousands of cars had rushed past, but how many had I really seen? How many could I identify by sight and actually say who owned it?

Only one. This one.

It really was a small world. Tight, sometimes. Parked

in the stall for that apartment was the limousine with the personalized license plate I would never forget:

STAR 1.

11

Life has a jagged sense of humor. Normally, I favor that quixotic, corkscrew brand of merriment, but I'd never before been on the receiving end of it quite so royally. I had achieved my lifelong ambition. I was a guest in my idol's lair — but I was only there to inflict the third degree on her.

Not that she wasn't enduring it well.

"But I don't know anyone named Phillip Chase," a serene Zoya Vrescu assured me.

Did I say a lair? Her apartment left mere elegance way behind it. Heaven should look so good. It was a dream setting of silks and sheens, with inlaid floors so magnificently crafted it would have been a crime to cover them, were it not with the foremost threads of the Orient.

Mind you, it was not intimate. How could it have been when the White House would easily have fit into it? That problem was overcome by its many clustered settings of velvet sofas and little chintz-covered chairs which looked like they belonged in museums, one of which held my humble form. And that outstanding, but sterile, collection was not alive — until Zoya entered it. I had expected that regal stage to overshadow her, but in Zoya's presence it became nothing more than a fitting background.

"Not Phillip, Philly," I said. "That's what he calls himself."

She shrugged disarmingly, as if to prove her point.

Up close, she was as handsome as I remembered. Her dark, curly hair was loose today and looked wildly tempestuous with her off-the-shoulder peasant-styled designer dress. She appeared incredibly exotic. It's hard to understand why men chase young girls and spurn women like Zoya. Did a little sagging along the jaw and a tiny collection of lines around the eyes put them off that much? There was certainly nothing else wrong with this woman that I could see.

I, of course, was another story. With my filthy, torn clothes, dusty backpack and bloody face, I looked like what she normally tossed out with the trash. But Zoya, classy lady that she was, never mentioned my appearance.

A maid with thick, quivering jowls, wearing a dour grey uniform, entered carrying a tray with tea service. I declined any refreshment but waited for Zoya to settle back on the sofa with hers.

"Phillip, Philly," she said in dismissal. "I still don't know him."

I bolstered my skepticism. Maintaining my hard-nosed detective persona became a struggle. Part of me was still her adoring, five-year-old fan. Part? Okay, most. My objectivity had my adoration pinned for the moment, but it was touch-and-go on the match.

"Ms. Vrescu, I know Philly Chase came to see you," I said and refreshed her memory with the circumstances.

"Yes, I remember that man. I just didn't recall his name, if I ever knew it."

She had an accent, but it was hard to place. I would not have said it sounded especially Eastern European, more generically continental.

I pushed a little harder. "Mind telling me why he was here?"

Apparently, she didn't. She wasn't objecting to this interrogation in the least.

"He said a friend of mine referred him to me. She's away just now, so I can't check. Not that it matters. He wanted to sell me something. An investment scheme." She frowned. "Real estate, I think. I referred him to my attorney. Just to get rid of him, you understand. I make all of my own investment decisions."

"Do you really?" Was I gushing?

"Of course. I'm nearly as good a businesswoman as I was a dancer. I just returned from a trip to Southern California, where I went to check on some of my holdings." Her smile sketched a failed attempt at humility. "When I was younger, I managed to pick up a few choice properties in Beverly Hills."

Zoya reached across the end table at her elbow for a small leather book, which she passed to me. It was a photo album, one of the purse-sized ones that many women her age fill with pictures of their grandchildren. Zoya's contained nothing but photos of properties. Most appeared to be New York buildings and covered the financial spectrum, but I spotted quite a number I recognized from home. She wasn't kidding when she described them as choice.

"You'll make plenty when you sell these," I said with

my usual finesse.

"Once I own something, I never let it go," Zoya assured me. She took a sip from her exquisite Limoges teacup. "Are you certain I can't get you anything?"

She was unexpectedly gracious, considering that I was a stranger who had forced my way into her home to beat her with a rubber hose, more or less. If Charlotte possessed a social veneer, this woman was glazed.

"Nothing, thank you." It was enough that she allowed someone who looked like a refugee from the sewer into her magnificent retreat without having to extend hospitality. Fortunately, I knew she had entertained someone just as shabby. "Ms. Vrescu, to return to the point, if you didn't know Philly Chase, why did you let him up here?"

"You see how I live," she said and gestured to her breathtaking background, as if it were a gulag. "I'm nearly a recluse. When someone promises a diversion, I can't resist. I'll let anyone in. I let you in, didn't I?"

"Doesn't that defeat the point of living in a secure building?" My tone took on more of a testy edge than I planned.

"Oh, I am a dangerous woman." She blushed and laughed. "I meant that I like living with danger, of course. My English . . . "

Her English was light-years better than Tony's. Who cared if she sometimes confused words as long as you could understand them?

Zoya placed her teacup on the table and pressed her hands together. "Now, Ms. Eaton, suppose you tell me the purpose of these questions."

She was still pleasant, but a hard glint of the sort that

must have given her command in those business confer-
ences in which she was such a killer appeared in her bitter-
sweet chocolate-colored eyes. I hadn't decided how much
I was going to tell her. To be honest, I hadn't thought
about it. Spur-of-the-moment decisions and letting the chips
fall *wherever* are more my style. It's not that I believe this
method to be better than thinking things through. And
sure, my life is always littered with chips. But I spare myself that awful emotional wrangling most people endure
before they end up making a spontaneous decision anyway. In the spur of this moment, I decided to spill the unabridged truth about Marisa's kidnapping.

"That poor girl," Zoya said.

The curtain of social poise momentarily parted to reveal the real emotions of the woman behind. Her sorrow
seemed a genuine, if excessive, display for the plight of a
stranger. But she was a great artist who undoubtedly felt
things deeply.

"To be held captive in a cold building." Zoya rubbed
her own bare arms with her hands.

"The nights *are* getting cold," I agreed.

"They are! Poor child." She shook her head in dismay
and poured more tea in her cup. "How much is the ransom, if you don't mind my asking? Will your family be
able to meet it?"

My lips twisted into a wry smile as I explained the
peculiar demand for Marisa's life.

"How very odd. You don't think . . . " Zoya's voice
became hushed and cautious. "I mean, Mr. Hunt is a promi-
nent man. He wouldn't . . . would he?"

I shrugged. "I personally believe anyone to be capable

of anything — given the right circumstances." I've proved that more times than I cared to count.

"How true." She studied me. "And what is it you're doing with this questioning? Do you seriously imagine you can rescue your sister-in-law?"

She didn't laugh. I was sure of that. So why did I feel as if she had? I squirmed uncomfortably, till the sound my jeans made against the chair cushion reminded me that I was probably rubbing motor oil on her froufrou chair.

"I'm looking into it," I said with poorly mustered dignity.

"I see." That she didn't believe I had a shred of hope was painfully apparent. "Is that wise? Anyone who would kidnap someone just to secure a restaurant is not a person to be crossed."

I shrugged. "Not to worry. I'm not good enough to die young." Any number of people would confirm that.

"On the contrary, my dear, I fear you are." Creases formed across Zoya's brow. "Is your family planning to pay the ransom? Assuming your . . . efforts don't work?"

"That decision hasn't been made — yet," I said. So much for the unabridged truth.

"The police haven't been notified?" Zoya rose and went to the wall, where she pressed against a small panel, discretely disguised by its grass-cloth wall covering, which opened to reveal an electronic thermostat. She made a slight adjustment to the room's perfect climate.

"Informing the police doesn't seem to be a consideration." I still shuddered when I remembered how the family surrounded me when I tried to make that call.

Zoya fixed me with a stern look. "In my life, I have

always found it to be a mistake to yield to tyranny."

"That stand is harder to take when the life of someone you love is at stake." Why was I defending the Eatons?

"Perhaps," she said, though she sounded unconvinced. She was made of sterner stuff than my in-laws, but Marisa wasn't her child.

Having covered what I'd come to ask and not enjoying being on the receiving end of her scrutiny, I attempted to close the interview. But Zoya seemed to want me to stay. On her way back to the sofa, she gave my arm a friendly brush.

"You know, Ms. Eaton — " She smiled in a way that suggested she was laughing at the formality we'd imposed on ourselves. "Tracy. May I call you Tracy? I'm Zoya, of course. Something about you is awfully familiar."

I bit back, *I'm the idiot at the airport who chased your limousine all the way to Manhattan*, and said instead, "I'm sure I would remember if we had met." Suave, huh?

"No, I know you from somewhere." She tapped her finger against her nose, while she thought about it, then snapped her fingers. "I'll be right back."

I was about to say she floated from the room, until I looked at the floor. A thick carpet covered this room. Like all ballet dancers, Zoya's feet were turned out, and while her body's excellent carriage gave the appearance of floating, her walk was awkward. Making it worse, she dragged her feet, as demonstrated by the impressions scraped into the carpet by her steps. I wasn't altogether sorry the dancing talent I wished for never materialized.

Flashing an impish grin, Zoya returned carrying a copy of one of my books, *You Can Take it With You*. She turned it around to reveal the photo on the back of the jacket.

"I would have recognized you sooner, but you're much lovelier in person," Zoya crooned.

Even I didn't believe that, especially after inspecting the floor of her garage at close range. The photographer who took that picture should win the Nobel Prize, if he wasn't outright canonized.

"Tracy, I couldn't put it down. It's so literate."

Now that's something a mystery writer doesn't often hear. I wasn't sure I liked it.

"If anyone can find your sister-in-law, I'm sure you can."

Her respect for my prowess as a detective had obviously risen now that she knew who I was. She was nearly gushing, or as close to it as a sophisticated creature like her came. I felt guilty for withholding my praise of her, but if I said anything now, it would sound like obligatory reciprocation. She opened the book's front cover and drew an affectionate finger over the blurb. I felt as if I were cheating her.

Fortunately, she didn't seem to want to discuss the book the way fans often do, so I was able to arrange a quick getaway. When I was about to step through the door, I remembered something else I'd wanted to ask.

"Zoya, I believe we also have a personal connection. Don't you know my mother-in-law, Charlotte Eaton?"

She thought for a moment, then shook her head. "I know many socialites." The curl of her lip showed what she thought of them. "But I don't believe I've ever met that one."

12

I floated from Zoya's apartment. Imagine . . . I was the idol of my idol. Okay, so maybe I wasn't exactly her *idol*, but she liked my stuff. She said so. And what a warm and gracious woman she was. While I'd always revered her talent, I envisioned her as haughty and unapproachable. I never expected such open gentility.

Not that I was letting the pleasantries scramble my brain. But Zoya's account of Philly's visit rang true, even if not everything our family scam artist did that afternoon made sense.

If he was only going out to practice his craft, as it were, why did he behave so secretively? The most important skill in a con man's arsenal had to be the ability to manufacture the appearance of innocence; creating the opposite impression served no purpose. I could understand his nervousness if he had been afraid of being observed by the police. But the police were there, and Philly couldn't have spotted them or he would not have gone on to peddle his flimflam real estate deal. Hell, they were so unobtrusive even I didn't notice them — and as many times as I'd written such scenes, I had to be good.

I wanted to go to The Gypsy Princess, but I desperately needed a shower and a change of clothing. Though I'd slipped into a ladies room before visiting Zoya for a touch of on-the-spot repair, I still reeked of *eau de petroleum*. I zipped back to the house. Once again, I ran into Drew, in the suite this time, stretched out on the black-and-grey bedspread and staring at the ceiling. If my understanding of the plan was correct, he should have been hunched over a phone in his father's office. How would I explain my appearance?

His eyes shifted absently in my direction, but he didn't seem to notice a thing when he greeted me. "Hey, Trace."

Though he seemed to be studying the ceiling of the room, the way he addressed me sounded like it might have when he and I were still *simpático*. I felt a lump forming in my throat, and I didn't know whether to let it grow or to beat it with a stick.

I shed my filthy clothing quickly, before he became more observant, and stuffed them into the bathroom hamper. I needed a shower, but Drew's lethargy bothered me. I snatched my paisley silk robe from the back of the bathroom door and returned to the bedroom.

"What are you doing here, Drew? I thought you were going to be working from your father's office."

He rolled onto his side and absently watched as I made choices for later at the open closet door. "Do you know what time it is in France? Care to guess how many Dumonts there are? I had to get away. Dad's demands for updates every five minutes were making me crazy. We're meeting Hunt later today. I said I'd see him there."

"How did Hunt sound?" I hooked a couple of hangers over the top of the door and turned back to Drew.

"Dad handled that call. He only told me about it as I was headed out the door. I thought I'd go out for a little walk, but somehow I ended up here."

That was not a *little* walk, but Drew didn't appear to notice. I found myself moving across the bedroom to be near him on the bed.

"I was just thinking about the very first time I saw her," he said. "Marisa, I mean. Did I ever tell you that story?"

He had, but I encouraged him to continue and sat on the bed beside him.

"When Dad told us his firm was sending him to Europe for a year and that he was taking Mom, we assumed we would go along. We couldn't believe it when they enrolled Corbett and me in a boarding school. They always said boarding schools were places wealthy people used to get rid of the kids they didn't want around — and there they were getting rid of us." Drew traced an aimless pattern on the surface of the spread. "To make it worse, the discipline at the school was so strict, it made a military academy look lax."

I doubted it had been that bad. Drew thrived on discipline. But I knew I would never convince him. He would always see it through the eyes of a wounded child.

"They arrived back in the States just before the end of school. Dad drove up to get us. We were a little surprised Mom wasn't there. On the way home, Dad explained they'd had a baby while they were away and that Mom was home taking care of the little bugger. A baby! We didn't want a baby. *I* was the baby. They hadn't even told us one was on the way. So it would be a surprise, they said. Some surprise."

He went back to staring at the ceiling, as if the past were projected there. Through the outrage building in his voice, I heard how much he resented the newcomer. As an only child, the area of sibling rivalry was a vast unknown to me, though my parents and I engaged in a facsimile of it.

"I despised the whole idea of a baby and knew nothing would change that," he continued on. "I'm ashamed to say it now, but all the way home I plotted the things I would do to her. You know, pinch her and stuff. We got back to the house, and there was Mom. She was so happy to see us and anxious for us to like the baby, I almost forgave her for leaving us. By then I blamed the whole thing on Marisa."

Unconsciously, I raked my fingers through his hair. Just as absently, Drew took my hand and held it. "So what happened to change that?" I asked.

"Mom made Corbett and me sit on the floor, and she put this little *thing* on its stomach on the floor between us. Marisa wasn't good at crawling, but she managed to slide over to me. She grabbed my finger. You know, the way babies do. And she gave me the biggest smile. She had hair — they'd told us Corbett and I were born bald. Dark hair, and it was curly. I thought she was the prettiest little thing I'd ever seen. In that moment, I became her big brother, and I vowed that I would take care of her for the rest of my life. That I would never let — "

He swallowed hard and turned away from me. It was pointless to tell him he hadn't let her down, he was sure he knew better.

I sensed he needed to be alone now and slipped away to the bathroom for my shower. But a question brought me back into the bedroom.

"Drew?"

He responded with a gruff grunt.

"At this school, you started around the beginning of September and ended in June, right? You weren't there for the summer session?" I asked.

"God, no! Why?"

"No reason."

∞

Since I hadn't managed to get all the dirt out from under my nails, I still felt like a mechanic. But the snappy red jumpsuit I wore helped to restore my spirits.

I stopped upstairs for a snack before taking off again. It wasn't hard to guess how Charlotte was purging her anxiety. Despite having had the house cleaned the day we arrived, she'd scrubbed the whole place herself this morning. The air was so lemon fresh, I nearly gagged.

Drew and his mother doubled-teamed me once more in the kitchen.

"Tracy, Martha called here again. She said you never returned her call," Charlotte said.

With my face buried in the refrigerator, I insisted I had, only Mother wasn't available. Let them prove otherwise.

Drew leaned into the refrigerator and brought his lips to my ear. "Can't you stay here with my mother? If she's left alone, she's going to strip the finish from all the furniture."

I slammed the refrigerator door shut and snatched an apple from a bowl on the table. "You know I'd love to stay here, Charlotte. Is there anything I like more than cleaning?" Sure — death, and maybe calling my mother. "But my bitch of an editor has me signing books now."

Drew stood with his arms crossed over his chest. "How is that possible? You told me your last book was going into paperback and — "

He listens to my grousing about my publisher? Why doesn't he ever hear when I ask him to take out the garbage?

"It is. But they found a bunch of hardcovers in the warehouse," I insisted. "And now they have me signing everywhere." That excuse should be good for a few unexplained getaways.

The instant I saw acceptance beginning to form on his face, I dashed from the room.

"Call your mother," Charlotte shouted after me.

Sure, that would happen.

13

Pleased with my progress, I decided I deserved some good transportation. I tracked down a working public phone and called Nuri, the terrific cabdriver I'd discovered the day before. I booked him for the rest of the day. Why had I left my cell phone at home? What made me think I wouldn't need it here? Lesson two for the new detective.

On the way to The Princess, a better starting place occurred to me, and I detoured Nuri to Marisa and Tony's Greenwich Village apartment. With a twinkle in his eyes and a wiggle of his moustache, Nuri insisted he wanted to share in my adventure. I waited until he could secure a parking spot — no small feat in Manhattan. But as we made our way down the corridor outside their apartment, I watched the veil of caution drop over Nuri's face.

"Tracy, are you sure about this? They are your family. What would they say if they knew what you were doing?"

If I'd known he was going to sound like Drew, I would have left him in the cab.

"How will you get in if you don't have a key? Are you going to pick the lock?" he whispered in a tone where disapproval struggled against excitement.

Warring factions tugged at Nuri. He struck me as a man who had spent most of his life following the rules. He'd taken some big risks lately. Some paid off, while others had not — I believed he was learning that risks added spice to his life either way. Sometimes he just wasn't sure.

I smiled enigmatically. I didn't know how I was going to get into the apartment, but I had a hunch. Amazingly, it paid off. At first glance, Marisa's apartment door didn't appear to be any different from those of her neighbors. A closer inspection revealed the apartment numbers were mounted on a slim plate that, while painted the same color as the door, was actually slightly elevated above its surface. I twisted the middle number — and the plate slid aside to reveal a small opening, cut into the door, that housed an extra key.

"That was mine at one time," I said in answer to Nuri's surprise. "It was on my door when my husband and I started dating."

"It's ingenious." Nuri couldn't resist trying to make the space appear and disappear.

"Don't know about that. It was designed by a friend of mine. He planned to market them — until it occurred to him that once the trick to working the gizmo became common knowledge, burglars would know it, too. When he gave up on the idea, I took the prototype. It was perfect for me; I was notorious for locking myself out. Still am."

"So why is it here instead of on the door of your home, Tracy?"

"Drew was convinced the trick to working it was obvious and swore he'd worry about my safety. I only agreed because he was such a nag. Anyway, Marisa was in that awful adolescent stage at the time, and she asked for it so she could lock her room at home without having to carry the key around. Kids — as if her parents couldn't figure out how the door plate worked. Anyway, I had a feeling she might still be using it."

I unlocked the door and slipped the key back into its cocoon. This had been Marisa's apartment before she met Tony. I wondered whether she'd shared the door's secret with him. Did he know how easily I was able to gain entry?

"What did you do about the problem of locking yourself out after you removed this device from your door?" Nuri asked.

"What I still do — I put the key under the mat."

With that piece of wisdom behind us, we entered the apartment; it was an average-sized place with an unusual design. In contrast to a small living room, an even smaller bedroom and a den that was little bigger than a closet, it featured a kitchen as large as the other three rooms combined. That was why Marisa picked it. The colors were the same as those of The Princess — Marisa's favorites — but this place had been decorated with a tighter budget.

I'd hoped to see signs of a struggle in the apartment. That would have provided a significant clue. It would have been apparent, too. The place was so neat, I wondered whether Charlotte zipped by for a quickie cleaning. Though I doubted my upper-class mother-in-law generally scrubbed floors, except as an antidote to anxiety.

My friendship with Drew's sister had been sealed by our shared love of books. Books filled that apartment. I left Nuri engrossed in reading the titles on the living room shelves, while I cased the rest of the room. But Nuri soon joined me with the intention of rattling his overdeveloped conscience in my face.

"I would feel guilty searching the home of a loved one," he said.

How restricting. While I copped to being a nosy person, I had my limits, too. Fortunately, I hadn't yet hit one. I once shook down my editor's office when she was called away during a meeting. Well, I figured she'd want me to bring that level of authenticity to my writing. No rationalizations were required this time. I knew Marisa expected me to do whatever I could for her. Tony might be another story, but that was the point. If he objected, I wanted to know why.

The problem was finding anything of Tony's. Their tastes must have been similar, since his contributions weren't easy to spot. Nothing fit with his background. Though her books had nearly doubled in number, all were written in English. I pulled several off the shelves and thumbed through them. It appeared that Marisa had bought an entire collection. The initials "J.A.B." were written on the fly-leaf of a number of them.

Their fabulous kitchen was equally unrevealing. Books also filled this room, but these were cookbooks. Ironically, there was little in the way of food in their big commercial refrigerator. Given the hours Tony and Marisa worked, it had to be hard for them to shop, not to mention indulging in the luxury of cooking just for themselves. Proving the point was a note Tony had left stuck to the brushed aluminum refrigerator door by a magnet shaped like a hamburger bun.

"Hey, babe," it read, "remind me to bring home some cream from the GP tonight, or we'll be having our coffee black tomorrow morning. Love ya, T."

I stuffed the note into my pocket.

∞

From there, we went to The Gypsy Princess. I had Nuri drop me off in the alley behind the building, and asked him to wait in the cab. This time I needed to be alone. I planned to use the key Tony had given me, but I didn't need it. A potato vendor had just finished loading the elevator with his delivery, and he held the door for me. Fortunately, that smiling man with ruddy cheeks didn't seem to be the chatty type. I needed that time to think.

I found my almost-brother-in-law slumped over the battered desk that nearly filled his tiny office, built into the storage loft over the kitchen. The stacks of overflow supplies it contained and the colorful Italian travel posters covering the walls made the office seem even tighter.

"*Buon giorno*, Tracy. Philly's buyer, he has been found?"

"Sorry, Tony, not the last I heard. Has the kidnapper called you today?"

He nodded frantically. "This morning. I do not think she believe me when I tell-a her Philly sell his share to stranger. A stranger we cannot find! She think we're stalling, but she agree to give us few days more. I am to receive another call then with final arrangements."

"That's great, Tony."

"It is-a not so great! What do a few days matter? That is still-a not enough time. I damn Philly. I regret the day Marisa ever suggest selling him a part of The Gypsy Princess." Tony closed his eyes and sighed deeply. "Oh, Tracy, my poor, darling Marisa. If anything happen to her . . . "

I reached across the desk and squeezed his hand. "It won't!" I said with more assurance than I felt.

"*Grazie.*" He tightened the muscles of his homely face to hold back the tears. "But I must-a not . . . how you say? . . . burden you."

"It isn't a burden," I insisted. "Sometimes talking helps. Tell me how you and Marisa met."

I could tell that talking wasn't a release for him but an effort, though worry had so eroded his strength he couldn't resist. He told me about the prestigious cooking school they'd attended in Florence and how they met cornering a cart that had run away with another student's *zuppa inglese.*

"That school sounds like something a friend of mine is looking for." I kept it casual when I asked for the precise address. Once I had it, I knew what to do with it. "Were the classes held in English or Italian?"

Tony hesitated.

"My friend will need to know that, Tony."

"*Sì,*" he said, rushing into speech, "Both, of course." For the first time, guile gripped his gentle face.

"Naturally. What was I thinking? Marisa knows no Italian, and at that time, I suppose, you spoke no English."

"Very little." Tony's eyes rocketed off the walls of the office, as if he'd noticed for the first time just how small that room was.

"You're doing well with it now. It won't be long before you're speaking like a native," I assured him.

His smile flickered nervously. You'd almost think the compliment didn't please him.

14

The following morning produced even more surprises. Now don't get me wrong, I love a good surprise. Even when I'm on the receiving end. But I'd learned to be wary when they came from Drew. When Mr. Straight became unpredictable, it was time to take cover.

"This was a good idea, Tracy," he said, when our destination came into view. "I'm glad we thought of it."

We? Drew had certainly experienced a radical change of heart about this outing.

"What do you mean I'm representing the restaurant co-op?" he demanded yesterday, after I dropped the bombshell. "Representing how?"

"Relax, Drew. I just promised Corbett you would fill in for him at their meeting tomorrow."

"Tracy, why didn't you tell me about this sooner?"

So he wouldn't have time to call his brother, of course, who by now might realize it wasn't entirely his idea. "I just forgot. Come on, sweetie, it relieved Corbett of one worry." Not to mention me. How else was I going to see all of those people?

Mulishly, he argued, "I don't know New York law

that well."

"So? You're licensed to practice here. Don't worry, they're not going to drag you before a judge. Think of yourself as representing your family. Don't you want to know what's going on in this organization?"

He agreed only grudgingly. Less than a day later, he thought so much of the idea, he was claiming credit for it. When Drew's opinions coincided with mine, he was up to something, just as I usually was.

The co-op meetings rotated among the members' restaurants. Today's was in The Fatted Calf. A British pub with "a warm, folksy atmosphere and aristocratic prices," according to the guidebook I'd bought yesterday to help me find my way around. We'd been walking at a good clip as we approached the restaurant, but Drew stalled a few doors away. He hadn't changed his mind, had he?

"Wait a minute, Tracy. Where's Philly? Didn't he say he was coming with us?" he asked.

"That's what he said, but he was already gone when I knocked on his door this morning. I guess he'll meet us, though it's funny he didn't leave a note."

Drew laughed shortly. He started to respond, but bit it back. Instead of the uncensored, he said, "As you said, Tracy, we're all a little forgetful just now."

Got to uphold that family honor — in front of the outsider. I hid the hurt beneath a smile that was getting tough to maintain.

Drew spotted the board members at the front of the restaurant and went to introduce himself. I snagged a bagel from the breakfast buffet assembled along one wall and found a table at the rear. I didn't know what to expect today, and I wanted to be in a position where I'd catch it all. The person who invested in The Princess must have had a reason. One of these days he or she was going to act on it. Maybe today.

No one there appeared threatening. Most of the restaurant owners sat alone at a table or with one or two others and didn't waste energy on anything more strenuous than eating and breathing. Restaurateurs keep late hours for early morning meetings. There were exceptions, though. One jaunty little man wearing a burgundy ascot buzzed from table to table like a bee in a flowerbed. Another mixer was an enormous man in his sixties, overweight but with a huge frame, pure white hair and a blotchy face.

Incongruously coupled with him was a tiny woman with hair dyed a pinkish blonde and a heavily freckled face. My finely honed people-watching skills told me the guy with the ascot was a social butterfly, but the big man and his little wife were lobbying.

As more of the co-op members filtered in, the big guy and his wife split up, each working part of the room. Though I tried, I never overheard a word of those conversations, but the faces were revealing. The odd couple, while struggling to hide it, were desperate. They weren't finding a receptive audience here.

When the big man passed my table, one board member spotted him and rushed to his side. "Dan, wait a minute, if you please," she said.

"Now, Nancy darlin', despite what you've heard, I take longer than a minute. Ask Edie. Or better — don't," he said with a lecherous chuckle. "Besides, the meeting's just about to start."

"It'll wait." With her steel grey hair and a strong face devoid of make up, this woman had a no-nonsense look that fit her direct manner.

"Save your breath, Nancy. That damn bank fouled up again, didn't it? I told the bank president if I couldn't count on them to process my checks right, they were going to lose one of their bigger customers."

He backed away, but Nancy stayed with him.

"Dan, please. Your dues are four months overdue. It isn't fair to the other members. So far, I've limited the information to the board, but I won't be able to keep it from the general membership much longer. We all go through rough patches, but we don't expect others to carry us."

"Some less than others," he said, his too-friendly mask slipping.

The tables were beginning to fill now, and I noticed most members tried to eavesdrop on that conversation.

"We can't wait any longer, Dan." You had to hand it to this Nancy. If she hadn't worked as a bill collector, she'd missed the opportunity of a lifetime. How many of us find such a perfect fit for our natural skills?

"Just wait to the end of the week, then I promise you'll be paid," Big-Dan said.

"Dan, I've heard that before."

"This time it's true, I swear it." Big-Dan wiped his forehead with a wilted handkerchief he yanked from his hip pocket. "I'm expecting some big money then. Real big."

The Gypsy Princess was scheduled to be sold soon. Coincidence? Big-Dan could have been blowing smoke. The chronically strapped will say anything for a few days' reprieve. That part of the conversation rang true. Were Big-

Dan and the little wife the third owners of The Princess? That might explain why Philly made himself scarce this morning. Now I wished I'd mingled instead of studying those people from the fringe and scarfing down bagels.

My miscalculation was brought home once the meeting started. Had I really considered these people to be half-asleep? They became so alert to what was being said, their collective tension pressed the air from that room.

A bald man in a white Cuban *guayabera* shirt ran the meeting in place of Marisa. He swept the routine business aside as if with a broom and went straight to what he called "the Hunt report." Corbett sent a letter to the board with Hunt's latest offer for The Gypsy Princess, as well as a detailed account of the veiled threat against the co-op that Hunt made orally to Corbett. Corbett's drunken account to his sister might have been lax, but there was nothing wrong with the work he'd put in writing.

They all spoke at once when the letter was read, some crying out for recognition, others making their case, shouting over others doing the same. The man in the *guayabera* called for order. Then he surprised us all by yielding the floor to Drew.

Drew's smile radiated warmth. Boy, were they in trouble. Drew could be charismatic as hell when he wanted. Usually, he preferred for his arguments to win on merit than emotional grounds, stickler that he was, but he was pulling all the stops today.

"You have my sympathy," he said. "Yours is such a tough decision."

His voice was passionate, sincere. The one he would have used as a trial lawyer had he not been seduced by the wacky world of probate law. Wholesale melting of juries would have been the order of the day.

"Especially since you've allowed yourselves to be painted into the corner by the brush of peer pressure," Drew continued.

The brush of peer pressure? When did he become so literary?

"What do we think when we see a person who allows false pride to stand between him and the greatest opportunity of his life? We may pity him, but we think he's a fool, especially when he gives that false pride the specious name, Principle. Why should it be any different with an organization?"

Tony slipped into the chair next to mine. "*Scusi*, Tracy," he whispered. "Why is Drew saying these things?"

I shrugged to Tony, but I was no longer perplexed. Now I understood what thoughts had prompted that long walk yesterday. Drew was trying to save his sister's life by sacrificing the co-op. To make Hunt, or whoever was behind the crime, so happy he'd spare Marisa. He was also trying to guarantee she would have a decent reputation within her industry when she returned. She wouldn't be the only one who fell to Hunt.

He was also violating every rule he'd ever set for himself, but that didn't seem important to him now.

Drew continued to spin his mesmerizing web. As a writer, I had to admire his use of language. He painted Hunt as their benefactor, provider of their greatest opportunity. But there were forces behind Hunt — that's what he called them, forces — that were too powerful for Hunt to control.

"If you don't care about yourselves, think about your families, your employees." Drew's voice vibrated with such righteousness, he could have led a revival meeting. "Will you be able to protect them against these forces? The violence may have already started. Only two days ago one of your waiters, Mr. Robert Arthur, was beaten severely enough to be hospitalized. Mr. Arthur claims his assailant was someone within the Hunt organization, though he's refused to identify the individual for fear of reprisals."

Drew had been a busy boy. If I hadn't locked him into attending this meeting, he would have found another way to make these arguments to these people. His presentation was too polished.

"That's true," agreed a woman whose stout body challenged the seams of her flowered dress. She obviously swallowed Drew's argument, though I suspected it had more to do with his dimples than his incisive reasoning. "Bob Arthur was supposed to work for me the night they put him into the hospital."

"Arthur is an unlucky gambler who gets knocked about regularly, love," a tall, skinny Englishman with a ponytail said. "He knows we threatened to sack him if he let his gambling interfere with his job again. He'd say anything to avoid that."

Drew frowned. It was getting away from him. He finished quicker than he probably intended by returning to the missed opportunity scenario, likening it to a chance to buy Xerox at a dollar a share. I couldn't see the similarity, unless they were now selling stocks with loaded guns.

Big-Dan leaped to his feet. "The lawyer is right. Why are we holding out? The agreement not to sell only benefits the most successful members. It's hell on most of us."

A chorus of mixed voices rang out, most in disagreement but with a few echoing wishy-washy approval. While Big-Dan struggled unsuccessfully to hold the floor, his wife studied every face in that room, cataloging the strength of their positions.

"What is wrong with you people?" Nancy, the stern bill collector, asked. "There's more at stake here than making a few bucks. If we sell Hunt our restaurants and open others, what will we do when he wants those? Are we going to hand over everything we care about for the rest of our lives?"

Drew wasn't making enough of a dent. I wanted to add my voice, but I didn't. While I knew he was wrong, I couldn't fight the big brother trying to keep a promise to a baby who once won his heart.

"How about our families?" asked an Asian man in a crisp yellow shirt and tattered jeans. "What if Bob Arthur really was beaten by Hunt's henchmen? Who'll be next? Maybe our suppliers, maybe our kids. Why don't we sell out now — while we still have something to sell?"

I leaned closer to Tony. "Has Hunt ever threatened any of you with physical harm before this?"

"Never." The admission was made with grudging honesty. "Is always just-a pressure to sell. Constant pressure."

Didn't make sense. Hunt was capable of violence. That so many of them accepted that he might have been behind their employee's beating was ample proof. But I'd never heard him accused of being stupid. If he was going to begin playing rough, why wouldn't he start with the type of random assaults on the co-op members that were easy to disavow, but so effective at weakening resolve, before leaping all the way to kidnapping?

Lord Hunt raised too many questions. I reviewed conversations I'd had with both Drew and his father last night after their meeting with Hunt. Naturally, Hunt claimed to be appalled that anyone would do something as brutal as abducting a lovely young woman like Marisa. But business was business, so he had no choice but to avail himself of the opportunity. The strange thing was he didn't question his good fortune. People, he insisted, often did him generous, if misguided, favors.

Well, Hunt could hardly admit it. What surprised me were the reactions he produced in my husband and father-in-law when I asked if they believed Hunt was guilty.

"We'd all like to think he's behind it, wouldn't we?" Drew asked. "Dad made sure Hunt understood that whoever took Marisa is safe from prosecution. Given that, he would be a fool to kill her. Yes, that's what we'd like to think."

"But you don't, Drew? Why?"

He shrugged. "Maybe because I sensed the whole business surprised him, though he didn't act it. That's what you'd expect — that he'd act surprised, if only as a way of proclaiming his innocence. Instead, he kept a tight rein on his emotions and let us do all the grandstanding. Still, I felt sure he was caught off-guard. But he weighed his options and seized the moment faster than anyone I've ever witnessed."

Taylor took a different view when I questioned him. "What does it matter what I think? Emotional wrangling might be a personal release, but it doesn't change the outcome."

That famous Eaton control struck again. "Taylor, just tell me what your gut says."

I thought he would refuse, until flames seemed to ignite in his golden eyes and the words burst from him. "My gut says he's guilty, of course. I'll tell you why, Tracy. Because I was afraid of him — and I'm not ashamed to admit it. Sitting together in his office, I felt as if I were locked in a cage with a hungry tiger who would claw through anything and anyone to get what he wanted."

A hungry tiger. I never expected such drama from Taylor. It was time I took a closer look at the man who produced those extreme reactions.

But first, just in case, I thought I might find me a whip and a chair.

15

"Hey!" I shouted. "The sidewalk's for pedestrians. Ride that thing in traffic!"

The bicycle messenger glanced back at me, but kept pedaling. Must have been his first day. Who else would try to ride a bike on that crowded sidewalk? So why was I the only one he hit? I rubbed at the mark left on the only remaining pair of jeans I had with me, but the greasy tire dirt would not come off.

The damage might have been worse. While a bike wasn't as dangerous as a car, I still might have been hurt if a quick-thinking man hadn't pulled me from its path. First, I was almost hit by a van, now grazed by a bike — and I'd done little to help myself in either case. I wasn't exactly being ignited by the pace of this fast-moving city.

But I was headed back to a slower time and a special place. A favorite haunt of my dad's when I was younger, The Stage Deli. He always took me there when we visited New York. We would slap loads of mustard on big, sloppy corned beef sandwiches and munch on Kosher pickles till we belched. One thing about Dad, he never lets fame rob him of the simple joys of ordinary life. Mother, of course, insists on it.

I took a booth with a view of the door at The Stage Deli. When a waitress arrived, I refused a menu and just asked for my old favorite. I ate all the pickles on the table while waiting for my sandwich to arrive. How were they? Beyond my ability to judge. You don't assess real estate on Memory Lane.

Despite the important place that restaurant held in my past, I wasn't able to give the experience all the attention it deserved. I kept thinking about Nuri, wondering whether I'd done the right thing.

∞

"Your husband's taste in clothes is . . . " It wasn't clear whether Nuri's inadequacy in English produced that struggle to find the right word — or tact.

"Dull," I offered. Drew always bought good clothes, generally the best the *frères* Brooks had to offer, but if I said they were trendy, my nose would grow a foot.

"No, Tracy." Nuri tossed his hand in a throwaway gesture, which struck me as very Old World in nature, though I'd never seen its like from Tony. It was a gesture that conveyed the complex thought: We will never speak of this, though we both know it's true.

The reason for Nuri's assessment of Drew's taste in clothes was that he stood before a mirror in our suite wearing one of Drew's suits — and it fit perfectly. I'd slipped him into the house right under Charlotte's nose. Nuri and his family escaped Iraq with little more than what they wore. He no longer owned what he needed to wear for this little caper. A trip to Drew's closet was in order, and what Drew didn't know would never cause me any pain. The trick to juggling is just keeping all the balls in the air.

I came up behind Nuri to check out his image in the mirror behind the closet door. With the joy of adventure clear on his face, he managed to look quite dashing in Drew's stodgy grey suit, crisp white shirt, and power red tie; even the tasseled black loafers fit him well, though he did say they were a bit snug.

"You're sure about doing this, Nuri? I haven't pushed you into it, have I?"

"Very sure, Tracy. This is nothing like the other."

"The other" was Nuri's euphemism for the spot of breaking and entering we pulled on Marisa's apartment. That merry spark surfaced in Nuri's eyes again.

"Good." I sighed, my relief too obvious.

Nuri hesitated and turned to me. "It isn't, is it, Tracy? Because you know, I am only a resident in this country. It's legal, what you want me to do?"

"Of course it's legal!" I insisted, scandalized. What had he heard?

"Then I will gladly do whatever I can to help you find your sister-in-law." Nuri admired his reflection again. "Who better? This is an area I know something about."

I really wasn't all that sure of its legality, preferring to remain vague on that subject, but I was certain no one would complain, which amounted to the same thing. Nuri's task was to find a little leverage that could be used against Lord Hunt. Posing as a wealthy Middle-Eastern business-man, he arranged a meeting with Hunt to discuss the pos-sibility of investing in one of Hunt's projects. Once they were face-to-face, Nuri would allow Hunt to understand his money might be of dubious origin. If Hunt agreed to take it anyway, I'd have something to use against him, since we would be taping every word.

The only part that bothered me was Hunt's choice of meeting location, a seedy bar on Eighth Avenue near the Port Authority Terminal.

"Why would a man with a perfectly good office want to meet in a bar?" I asked, after smuggling both Nuri and the suit from the house. Especially one in a dangerous neighborhood with so many sleazy, adult businesses.

"Perhaps he is merely casual. I have observed that many people in this country are quite casual."

"When you're here longer, Nuri, you'll appreciate the difference between casual and offensive." I didn't like it; I was responsible for Nuri. Still, the implications were good for what I hoped to accomplish. Why would Hunt assume Nuri's business was shady?

∞

The worry continued to gnaw at me during my time in The Stage Deli, so much so that it took me nearly five minutes to polish off my corned beef sandwich. Well, I owed it to Dad to make the effort. My biggest fear was that I'd miscalculated about Hunt. It seemed a good idea to send Nuri in first to gather the shakedown material, so I hadn't had a chance to form my own impression. I realized I had been operating under the premise that Hunt was semi-bent and planned to use that — but what if he were thoroughly twisted? Would Nuri be able to handle it?

I considered taking a stroll past the bar where Nuri and Hunt were meeting, even if it meant adding strangers with an interest in my sex life to my circle of acquaintances. But Nuri walked through the door. He slid into the booth across from me, loosened Drew's power red tie and unbuttoned his collar.

"That was awful." He released a flood of tension with one great sigh. "And it was wonderful." He grinned broadly.

How ya gonna keep 'em down on the farm? "Well?" I demanded. I wasn't known for my patience.

"It was . . . interesting. I made sure he understood the investment came from a questionable source — and he didn't care."

"He said that? And you got it on tape? That's great, Nuri. Exactly what I hoped for."

Nuri signaled for the waitress and asked for a cheese sandwich and a Coke. "Yes, the man is quite indifferent to the source of the money invested in his company. That part went very well." Nuri paused. "*That* was not where I lost him."

I didn't need to be hit with a brick. "Where did you lose him?"

"I'll play that part of the tape for you." He took from his pocket the tiny recorder I'd swiped from Drew's suitcase and fast-forwarded. "Listen to this."

An unfamiliar voice asked, "What kind of turnaround are you looking for?"

Nuri hesitated, then continued with confidence, "What I want is a fairly long-term investment. Through construction. But I would probably like to stay on until the building is several years old."

"I see," Hunt said.

I could hear him pulling away. He obviously did see something I missed. I understood Nuri had blown it over that turnaround time, but had no idea how.

He switched off the recorder. "I tell you something, Tracy. I was an architect before I came here. I know builders." He paused, then continued forcefully. "I don't know what this man, Hunt, is — but I know he is not what he *says* he is."

∽

Nuri's words echoed in my mind all evening. I listened to the whole tape repeatedly. I'd been afraid Nuri might have tried to hook Hunt into some esoteric construction conversation in which Hunt simply hadn't chosen to engage, but it wasn't that at all. He merely asked the type of questions anyone investing in a project would ask. It was clear Hunt didn't know squat about the business that was supposed to be the source of his fortune.

The walls of the Eaton home, and the pain trapped within them, were smothering me. I needed to take a walk, do some thinking. I slipped on my navy blazer and sneaked out when Drew and his parents were arguing in the living room. I closed the front door with a soft click. Though for once, it wasn't necessary to hide that I was leaving. Drew was avoiding me tonight with such determination that you'd think I was a carrier of the plague instead of just ulcers, as he usually maintained.

The reason for the silent treatment escaped me at first. Finally, I understood. I wasn't the culprit — he was. He felt so guilty about his actions at the restaurant co-op meeting, he couldn't face me. But dammit, I wasn't his conscience. He had no right to do this to me.

Before I left the house, I had called the number where Taylor said Corbett was staying in France. The man who answered roared into the phone. The voice was thick with sleep or maybe booze, but it sounded like Corbett. At least that was something I didn't need to worry about.

During my walk to Central Park, I remained in an awful funk. I knew going into the park after dark wasn't considered to be the wisest of diversions, but to borrow Zoya Vrescu's phrase, I was a dangerous woman. In my present mood, the muggers had more to fear from me.

I didn't know how long I walked. I'd done my best to blank out all thought for a while. Obviously, I succeeded; the sound of someone coming up behind me never registered. By the time he slipped a strong arm around my neck and touched the point of his knife to my cheek, it was too late.

"Okay, sweetheart, now be a good girl, and you'll leave here a little poorer but alive. Got that?"

I said I did, and he released me. I turned to face my attacker. He'd chosen a poorly lit section of the path, but we could see each other well enough. My mugger was such a hunk, he should have been smiling from the pages of GQ, not knifing people in Central Park. Not that I found his attributes all that stirring.

"Give me your money and your jewelry."

His eyes dropped to my left hand, as if he expected to see a ring there. When he didn't, it disconcerted him for an instant. I might be foolish enough to roam around a park that was too big for the police to adequately patrol, but this wasn't my first day in the world. I'd left my jewelry at home, and I had taken the precaution of arming myself. In a manner of speaking.

"Now!" he ordered. "And maybe I won't have to hurt you."

He would anyway. I could see that in his eyes. There was nothing to be gained by making it easy for him.

I took a small step back, then another. The mugger jerked the knife a little closer to discourage me from running away. That wasn't my intention — I wasn't finished here. I slipped both of my hands into my jacket pockets, then pulled out the left holding a fifty-dollar bill. I kept my arm close to my body. He reached for the bill; because of the distance I'd placed between us, he had to lean forward. While he was in that unbalanced state, I yanked from my right pocket a sock filled with quarters. Man, that puppy was heavy. When the sock connected with his arm, the knife sailed into the bushes. Then I went for his head.

Much as I dread lapsing into cliché, there's no other way to say it: Something really did snap in me. Blame it on the tension or my anger with Drew and his parents. Before I knew it, I had that scumbag flat on his back and was flailing away at him.

"Not the face! Not in the face! Not in the face!" he cried.

Barely listening, I just kept swinging, and all he could do was occasionally deflect a blow with his arms. I was unstoppable — except by an outside force, which was what brought our fracas to a halt.

A man out for an evening run suddenly grabbed my

arms and pulled me to my feet.

"Okay, lady, that's enough," he said. "Give the guy a break."

"Give *him* a break? He was mugging me."

"Yeah, that's how it looked." The runner helped my attacker to his feet. "You okay, pal?"

Pal didn't answer. He just turned his bloodied face and ran as fast as a gazelle.

"Usually, I advise women alone to stay out of the park at night," the runner said before jogging away. "But you can take care of yourself." It didn't sound like a compliment.

It also wasn't true. I doubted whether my self-defense tactics would work as well with a real mugger. Right — he was no more a mugger than I was, despite what that runner thought about me. It was too much of a coincidence to believe the man robbing me in Central Park tonight was the same man who tried to run me down with his bike this afternoon. If I had to guess at his profession, I'd say he was neither a thief nor a deliveryman but an out-of-work actor or model. How many men care more for their faces than their lives?

When I'd looked into his eyes, I knew his threat to hurt me was real. But they weren't the eyes of a psycho, just a man steeling himself to perform an unpleasant chore. A chore he'd been hired to perform.

Someone wanted me out of action. Not permanently, just until after the sale of The Gypsy Princess. Someone thought I knew more than I did.

But who?

16

"Charlotte, I don't think Philly slept in his bed last night," I said the next morning, having cornered Charlotte while she carried a stack of clean towels between the laundry room and the linen closet.

"Did you check the doorway, dear? He probably felt more at home there." Her eyes widened in shock at her own remark. "Tracy, what you must think of us. I'm sorry, dear, but difficult times do bring out the worst in people, don't they?"

I understood. She wasn't really disturbed by what she said, merely that she said it to me. I shoved my bruised feelings aside and tried to bring her back to the subject.

"No one has seen Philly in over a day. I think — "

She cut me off with a weary sigh. "Tracy, surely you can see it's better this way."

What way? Giving up on Charlotte, I nailed Taylor while he sipped his morning coffee and skimmed the paper in the den.

"It's for the best, Tracy," was his cliché.

Who died? Someone must have generated those good wishes for the final journey, and don't let the door hit you when you leave. My last hope was Drew. I trapped him in the kitchen, where I found him peeling an orange.

"Drew, Philly is missing."

Before I could utter another sound, he hurled the orange into the sink and shoved me into the pantry.

"Leave it, Tracy!" The muscle beneath his left eye throbbed wildly. Not good. When that level of pressure entered the picture, Drew became even more tight-assed than usual.

"Drew, I'm just trying to help." I shifted a little; a box of spaghetti dug into my side.

Drew must have thought I was trying to escape; he blocked the door. "You create more problems with your help than other people do with world wars. Leave it alone, Tracy. Philly is a big boy, free to come and go as he pleases." Suddenly, his face paled; the twitch went nuts. "Oh, no! Tell me, Tracy, that you aren't . . . doing it."

"Doing it?" When my beloved displayed all the warmth of Attila the Hun?

"You know what I mean!" he shouted.

"Well, most people think 'doing it' means — "

"You are not most people, Tracy! You have obsessed on one thing for all the years you've been writing. And if ever there was an opportunity — " He stopped and closed his eyes; probably counting to ten. "Swear to me — *please* — that you are not playing detective."

Was that all? "I swear." *Playing?*

"Thank God!" He became generous with his forgiveness but eager to remove his contours from mine. He eased the door open. "I know you mean well, Tracy, but believe me, Philly won't thank you for bringing his absence to everyone's attention."

"He might not be able to," I said to myself. Drew had already flown the food coop.

This situation was beyond my comprehension. I wouldn't expect anyone to worry about Philly's absence, given his proclivities. But one member of this family had already been abducted. When a second went missing, it should have at least produced concern, not relief. Even if Philly had departed of his own accord, didn't anyone want to know why?

Disgusted with the family's reactions to Philly's disappearance, I took my leave before breakfast. Good choice. My buddy, Detective Billy Jay Weaver, sent some patrolman — who looked like he wasn't old enough to shave — to pick me up. Fortunately, he hadn't made it to the door — just yet. That was all I would have needed, a patrolman at the Eatons' doorbell. After Charlotte got over her palpitations at what the neighbors would think, she'd start suspecting me!

Officer Costas had orders to take me back to Weaver's office downtown. Such a long drive could have killed the morning. Luckily, the baby-faced Costas enjoyed showing me how the siren worked. Sometimes it's just so easy.

∞

The first thing I noticed about Weaver's desk was how messy it looked today. Since I'd never known one of those anal types to leap the neatness gap, I questioned his metamorphosis.

"We've got to stop meeting like this," I said.

Weaver looked like he thought a hotshot author should have been able to come up with something better. Let's see what he could do before coffee.

"So, Ms. Eaton, anything new with Philly?" He leaned back in his squeaky chair and propped his feet on that messy desk. His manner was congenial, but he didn't apologize for dragging me there.

"Lost him, huh, Weaver?"

His silence was response enough.

"I will if you will," I said.

He didn't plead ignorance; he accepted with a reluctant shrug. I honestly hadn't expected him to agree. Now I had to find something to give him.

"He's missing," I said, fulfilling my part of the arrangement.

"I knew that!"

"No, you didn't. You might have suspected, but you didn't know it, or you wouldn't have brought me in." I filled him in on the little I knew of Philly's disappearance, stretching it out so that it sounded like more than it was. I didn't think it fooled him. "Now — your turn."

"For that little bit of information, I don't think I owe you anything. But . . . " He surveyed the office; the only one of his officemates present was engrossed in a phone call. " . . . what do you want to know?"

"Whatever you've got."

"Them Eatons don't just hide the skeletons, they hide whole closets from the in-laws," he said with a chuckle.

This time it was my silence that spoke volumes.

"Philly Chase isn't as bad as most we see in here. Many of his schemes aren't outright cons, they're just dubious investments. I expect Philly is one of those people who can convince himself of anything. There's not much harm in him but not much sense, either. I'm just glad he doesn't get home too often. He prefers working in Europe. Maybe the language barriers make his swindles sound better."

I knew that lovable little corkscrew couldn't be completely crooked. There was a contradiction here.

"If Philly isn't engaging in some big deal larceny scheme, why have you been wasting manpower keeping tabs on him?" I asked.

He hesitated, then relented. "We had a tip Philly was moving up to the big leagues, and he'd picked himself a real important mark."

"I thought you said Philly wasn't seriously fraudulent."

"Old news, Ms. Eaton. Looks like the future might be a little different."

"Who is this mark?" I asked.

"Lord Hunt."

Hunt — again? I stared out the window, trying to put it together. Weaver's squad room had the best view; you could see both the Brooklyn and Manhattan Bridges from it. Anywhere else I would have planted myself at the window for some serious gawking. Other concerns overshadowed it here. No wonder Philly made himself scarce. The implications of Weaver's remarks made my head spin. Somehow, I had to get him off Philly's back. I needed to find a way to handle this.

"I think you should consider your source. From the little I've seen of the man, Hunt is light-years beyond Philly's orbit." Did Philly know that?

"I told you he was moving up, Ms. Eaton."

"He'd never make it through the door."

I prided myself on the natural sound of my insistence. I truly was my parents' offspring, but I reserved my histrionic skills for a more pressing arena. I didn't believe a word of what I'd said. I feared Marisa's kidnapping was payback for some move Philly had already made. I didn't want to believe Philly would put Marisa through this ordeal, but he was no tower of strength.

"They both might surprise you," Weaver offered.

No kidding. While I debated what to feed Weaver to divert him, he acted as if he'd forgotten something.

"Damn! Now where was . . .?" he muttered in agitation, while sifting through the clutter on his desk. He found a manila envelope in the disorder, issued a perfunctory apology for his departure, and dashed from the office. Leaving me alone with all his stuff. Silly man.

17

I couldn't believe Weaver would be so careless as to leave me alone at his desk, but everybody makes mistakes. I looked over my shoulder and saw the other detective had left sometime during my conversation with Weaver. Now was my chance. Before I could get down to any serious snooping, however, I heard the sound of approaching footsteps.

"Jay, I — " a woman's voice began, but stopped when she saw me alone at Weaver's desk. "Excuse me, I didn't realize there was anyone here."

I turned — and felt my jaw drop in shock all the way to my breastbone. "You're Leila . . . "

I shouldn't have said "Leila," I should have said, "LEILA!"

Weaver's wife, whom I had dismissed as "little Leila from Arkansas," was none other than *the* LEILA — no last name — whose face had probably graced more magazine covers than any supermodel in a decade. I couldn't believe it. Nor could I bear to be polite. I snatched her picture from Weaver's desk and gawked in disbelief. It had to be the only bad picture she'd ever taken. The punishing glare of the sun had flattened her fabulous bones; her face looked washed out and plain. Probably shot it himself, proving he was not only a wretched photographer but a sneaky man. Was this the way Weaver saw her, or did he just like not having her recognized?

"Yes, I'm Leila Weaver." She offered me a friendly smile — and looked fabulous, even when she wasn't trying. She wore the most marvelous camel-colored cashmere suit with matching accessories. Jeez, I felt like an absolute slob in her presence.

"He never said," I sputtered — finally.

"He never does," she said with an elegant shrug, apparently content with his choice.

Her voice was only about half as honeyed as Weaver's, and she seemed more in sync with the Northeastern pace he griped about. She'd have to be, since she was one of *the* trendsetters of the Western World. It looked like Weaver's dream of returning to the South was of the pipe variety.

"I recognized you, too, Ms. Eaton." Leila pulled a copy of my last book from a swank leather tote bag she carried and asked me to sign it. "Jay told me he'd met you."

"Jay?" I asked, gawking at the Billy Jay nameplate.

Leila smiled pleasantly, but I could tell she thought I should have been able to see through her husband's good ol' boy act. I had seen through it, I wanted to protest. I just didn't realize it extended to his name. I was really sinking in the Weavers' expectations.

I picked up a pen from bubba Billy Jay's desk and inscribed a "thank you" to Leila for being a devoted reader and signed my name with a flourish.

Leila shyly accepted her book back, if you can believe

it. "I think we've read all of your books, Ms. Eaton. Jay really loves 'em."

"Please call me Tracy," I said with gratitude.

So — Weaver lied. I said he was sneaky. Of course, there was an implied insult there. The source of my greatest pride was something Weaver felt he had to hide. But I understood. He wouldn't be able to pound the suspect into the ground if she had a box to stand on. Now we were equals; I might even have a slight advantage. I couldn't be happier if the bank made an error in my favor — even with a bunch of zeros. Well, maybe I could.

∞

"Friend o' yours?" Weaver asked, leaning over my shoulder.

Damn, caught! I knew when Leila had taken her leave that too much time had passed to engage in any serious snooping, but I did it anyway. What came over me? Besides the irresistible pull of my true nature. It was that copy of a mug shot on the desk. During Weaver's search for his envelope, it had been pushed in front of me. How could I not study it?

The picture was of a big woman maybe in her fifties, overweight, but more largely boned and heavily muscled than fat. There's nothing more grim than an arrest photo, but this woman managed to inject a smirk into hers with the slight, upward tug of one side of her mouth. The smirk only added to the message sent by her eyes — that anyone who crossed her would end up dead. And, surprise, surprise — she was also the same woman who nearly ran me over with a van the morning Marisa was kidnapped.

Funny, but when Corbett asked if I would recognize her if I saw her again, I couldn't remember how she looked. Now I knew her in a flash. Still, this picture produced none of that sense of familiarity that the brief sighting of the living person had. Perhaps that recognition required three dimensions and malice aforethought injected into her ugly kisser, but more likely the whole sensation was just a function of my imagination. My leap from the jaws of death just caused a few electrical impulses to go awry.

"I asked if she was a friend of yours?" He repeated the question pleasantly when he took his squeaky chair, but with growing insistence. The sugar coating wasn't all washed off, but I was beginning to taste the pill's bitter center.

I grasped the significance of Weaver's sudden transformation to a slob. The mess on the desk, his unexpected departure, the mug shot tossed in exactly that position — those things were staged. He *wanted* me to see it.

"You looked like you might have recognized her," he added, way too casually.

He thought I knew her! He couldn't have learned this woman almost ran me down. The incident only lasted a moment, and I hadn't told anyone outside the family.

"I don't know her. She looks so tough, I don't think I'd want to know her."

That was putting it mildly. I remembered her as having red hair, but I would have guessed that from this copy, though it was black and white. Pronounced freckles dotted her face, as they often do with redheads. Not that the freckles made her look wholesome. It looked like her face had taken a load of buckshot and it hadn't fazed her.

"Tough? She is that," Weaver agreed. He settled back in his chair and beamed benevolently at me. "But don't you think there's something intriguing about her?"

She was about as intriguing as salmonella, but I couldn't say that. If I wanted to win anything in Weaver's game, I was obviously going to have to play it by his rules.

"What's her name?" I asked, feeding him what I thought must be the next line in the script.

"Belle Cannon." Weaver watched as a couple of the other detectives in the squad returned to their desks.

"And what did Ms. Cannon do to win this glamour photo session with the NYPD's very own photographer?"

Weaver looked at me, thinking. After a moment, he slapped his thighs with his hands. "Ms. Eaton, how'd you like to take a walk?"

∞

I'll play along with anything, especially if it gets me what I want. I figured Weaver's little game would yield something good; I just had no idea what. One Police Plaza was just a short walk from the South Street Seaport, an attraction popular with tourists and locals alike. Weaver didn't say much as we walked there, except to occasionally point out places that might be of interest to me as an out-of-towner. I felt like shaking him. But I let him play the game his way.

When we passed a hot dog cart, Weaver offered to buy me one. I hadn't had coffee yet, but what the hell?

He took a big bite of his hot dog. "Nothing like New

York 'dawgs.'"

Yeah, yeah — get on with it. Neither of us said another word, until we found a bench and sat staring out at the river, as if nothing might be happening there.

I couldn't stand it anymore. "Belle Cannon? What did she do?"

"Well now, Ms. Eaton, that depends on who you talk to. I can tell you she was indicted on murder one, but the jury never had its say on the matter. Ol' Belle took a powder before it ever got to that point."

How did any of this relate to me?

Weaver tossed pieces from his hot dog bun to the pigeons. "Belle was never what you would call a model citizen, but her record was no more'n a shadow compared to that of her late husband, Lou. Though Lou had his chance to go straight. During his first parole, he got a real job working for Lord Hunt."

Hunt again? Was Weaver baiting me? He couldn't know about Marisa? The Eatons would rather have had their tongues cut out than spill that news. Of course, there was one among them who would have blabbed long before the knife appeared. Was Weaver's interest in Philly's disappearance a ruse? Maybe the reason no one had seen that lovable old grifter lately was that he was languishing in the very same holding room in which I had once been housed. Maybe he was even reading the flight magazine I left behind.

"Yes, ma'am, Hunt gave Lou Cannon a chance to go straight. But Lou always fell off the wagon and returned to the joint. 'Course, whenever he got out, Hunt always had Lou's job waiting for him."

"Hunt must be either generous or an idiot," I said.

"Must be that Hunt's generous. No one's ever said that ol' feller don't have all his cornflakes in one box. 'Course it's probably a coincidence that Lou's crimes always seemed to aid Hunt's business and that Hunt paid Lou real well." When he finished feeding the pigeons, Weaver scooped a few pieces of gravel into his hand to skip across the water. "When cancer struck Lou, Mr. Hunt supported the Cannons through that last awful year of Lou's life."

No, he didn't have Philly, I decided. Weaver didn't even care much about him. That was just an excuse to pull me in and tell me this story. Why did he want me to hear it?

"How touching. Where does Belle come in?" I asked.

"Well, as you might imagine, Belle, she was real grateful to Lord Hunt. When a competitor managed to snatch a land deal away from Hunt, Belle up an' shot him. The competitor, I mean, not Hunt. Then Hunt turned 'round and bought the land from the heirs, who weren't about to reject Hunt's offer after what happened to their daddy. Belle was indicted for the murder, but she jumped bail before it came to trial."

"What about Hunt? How was it that he stayed in the clear? Surely he was involved." The hot dog sank like a piece of lead in my stomach.

"Think so? Hunt, he was shocked, of course, but he said it wasn't his fault a zealous friend wanted to do him a favor. Naturally, no one has ever proven otherwise."

That was the same as his reaction to Marisa's kidnapping. People were uncommonly generous to this man — too bad they supported that generosity with major crimes.

"So, you see, Ms. Eaton, if you spot ol' Belle coming

your way, you run like hell in the other direction."

"She won't be coming my way." That was my fervent hope. One encounter with Belle was enough.

"We don't usually have any control over the actions of other people," Weaver said.

"Weaver, she won't be coming my way. We don't know each other." I channeled my annoyance into hurling my napkin at a trash container.

"Of course not."

He still didn't believe me. Wasn't it ironic? I doubted whether I'd ever been this scrupulously honest in my life. I was better off lying.

Why did he think I knew this Cannon woman? Even if he heard about the incident with the van, it wasn't enough of a thread to have woven this cloth. Did he believe I could lead him to Belle? I sensed finding her wasn't what was going on here. Weaver was putting a puzzle together. He was willing to show me some of the pieces he had in hopes I'd lead him to those that were still missing. I listened because I had a puzzle of my own. But I was tired of playing by Weaver's rules. I cut to the quick.

"Detective, was that the case that got you tossed out of Homicide?"

He smiled slyly, not surprised that I knew, darn it. "I didn't get tossed out of Homicide; there was simply a 'shifting of personnel.' "

His tone was drier than the Sahara. You could hear the quotation marks.

"Still, it was my last Homicide case. I made the case against Belle, I tracked her down, and I arrested her. But you want to know a secret?"

Nodding, I found I wanted to know it badly.

"When you been a cop for a long time, you develop a sixth sense about people. I can't prove it, though God knows I tried, but I don't believe Belle killed that man. She set up the hit, mind you, but she didn't pull the trigger."

"Then — who did?" I asked, my voice scarcely above a whisper.

He shrugged. "You just might want to ask yourself who benefitted from it?"

Who benefitted? Hunt benefitted. Was he telling me that *Hunt* pulled that trigger?

It was time I found out.

18

Lord Hunt in the flesh just blew me away.

No, that's not to say he shot me — bite your tongue. It was that seeing him face-to-face in his office shattered my expectations. The job performed by his public relations staff was no less a feat of engineering than the high-rise buildings his company built.

Remember those pictures that have appeared in all the magazines, the ones with Hunt breathing down the neck of some influential person? Totally staged. Breathing *up* was the best he could hope for. He was a much smaller man than I expected. Maybe just eye-level with me, and I'm not that tall. And those photographs that capture him in the middle of a forceful stride? Faked again. One of his legs was shorter than the other and twisted out, requiring him to wear something that, despite valiant efforts to disguise it, was a built-up shoe that he dragged behind him.

Another area where my expectation was off the mark was in the depth of his social veneer. I thought the polish would sparkle. It didn't. There was a little of the sort of gloss that money imbues on everyone who possesses it, but it wasn't even skin deep. Without wealth's reflection,

Hunt would have looked like nothing more than a hood. He didn't look like much more anyway. A street thug made good, who mimicked the manner of a businessman. That handmade suit he wore must have cost five thousand dollars, but it would not have surprised me to learn he kept a knife in his sock.

Still, finding him to be less than the suave giant I'd expected wasn't the signal to rejoice. What we had here was not a lightweight. There was such a feeling of power about the man, yet brutality infused it. I'd come prepared to face Taylor's hungry tiger, only to encounter a rattlesnake. Either could kill me.

That wasn't merely a writer's fanciful impression. Mounted on the walls were the heads of animals he'd killed. I didn't think there was anywhere left in the world where endangered species could be hunted for sport, but Hunt's level of wealth answered many objections.

As if that weren't enough, another key aspect of the office's decor were the guns he'd used to kill those animals. An array of handguns and rifles filled four rosewood and lead-glass gun cases. Most looked more like the hardware favored by terrorists and cops raiding crack houses than hunters. Or what the infamous lone gunman might use to take out a watermelon at five hundred yards. What did I know? Guns don't play a big role in my mysteries. One of the cabinet doors was ajar, while the others were streaked with greasy fingerprints. He must have opened them often, lovingly caressing the killing objects within.

Why did this shock me? I'd been listening to his voice on tape, and for once, it fit. It sounded coarse, despite a spotty application of grammar. The voice of a man that, while completely lacking in subtlety, was probably as twisted as a Byzantine maze.

I flashed back to Weaver's implication that Hunt pulled the trigger on a competitor. Even if I had only met him apart from his telling surroundings, I would still have believed it.

What was I doing there? Funny, that was also what he wanted to know.

"Well?" the killer demanded.

Time to put up or shut up. Or maybe run for cover. "Mr. Hunt, I — "

He held up a hand like he wanted me to stop in the name of love. "Hold it. What is it you said you did again?"

Again? Considering the only sound I'd uttered for his hearing went into his receptionist's ear, we could hardly be said to have had this conversation before.

"I didn't — but I'm a writer."

"Yeah? Whataya write?" he asked.

I tried to decide whether he was serious about not knowing anything about me. If he staged this scheme, wouldn't he have taken the trouble to learn about Marisa's family?

"I'm the author of the Tessa Graham Mystery Series."

"Never heard of it."

As I said, no subtlety. I wouldn't get the usual "I don't read much" from this guy, or even the "I don't like genre fiction" snub. I sensed he dismissed me as an opponent because he classified my profession as a mental one. We thinkers can't act, right? We'd see about that.

"Now go ahead — whataya want?" he demanded.

Not so fast, little god. He might be used to sweeping

people out the door, but contrary to rumors, I don't ride on brooms.

"Mr. Hunt, I'm not the third owner of The Gypsy Princess," I said.

"Huh? Why the hell did you say you were?"

I figured that ploy would get his attention. I had to say something. I thought he'd be fortified behind layers of assistants and maybe even a moat or two. Go figure. One receptionist and not a moat in sight. I didn't even have to lie convincingly, dammit, and I always looked forward to that.

Hunt's operation was remarkably small for the headquarters of an empire. He had taken the top floor of his poshest building for his own address. And the private elevator did open into a waiting room with such a sumptuous carpet, it needed to be mowed. But I doubted whether there were more than three or four rooms to the whole suite.

I said as much to an indifferent receptionist obviously chosen more for the size of her bazongas than her telephone skills. With a superior smile of well-capped teeth over a badly bobbed nose, the blonde floozy explained they subcontracted a lot. Criminal understatement, to say the least. With such small overhead, no wonder Hunt was filthy rich.

I kept remembering Nuri's conclusion that Hunt wasn't a builder. So what did he do? The money hadn't been delivered by the stork.

"I'm a busy man, you know." He swept a hand over the smooth, uncluttered surface of his rich rosewood desk, as if he were sweeping away piles of work.

He gave the impression of someone who had nothing better to do. Maybe that was the secret of empire building, making it look easy. And knocking off the competition.

"Sure you are. But you want The Gypsy Princess, and we can't get it for you till we find the third owner. To do that, we need more information," I said.

He flexed his skinny shoulders. "You think you're going to get it here? I didn't snatch the kid. I told your old man that." His tone sounded closer to indifference than indignation. "It's not my problem."

His eyes, the same shade of green as the algae you see at the bottom of a pond, drifted as he spoke; not evasively, but like someone with a short attention span. I bored him. If this was an act, he could give acting lessons to Mother and Dad. He had enough discipline to bring his eyes back to mine occasionally, but only just.

I inched forward on a guest chair that probably cost more than my condo at home but which wasn't as comfortable as Weaver's old wooden one. "If we don't find the information we need somewhere, you don't get the restaurant."

"And you don't get your sister-in-law back, lady."

I brought my hand down on his empty desk. "Then you *really* don't get the restaurant, Mr. Hunt."

I still didn't understand why he wanted restaurants, but now I guessed his obsession with The Princess had more to do with Marisa's refusal to sell than any interest he had in owning it.

Idly, Hunt turned his head from side to side, as he seemed to weigh his options. "Call me Lord, why don't ya?"

I almost blew it by giggling. What was the matter with me? I knew his name, I just never imagined anyone using the stupid thing.

"Thanks . . . Lord." I felt like I was saying grace.

"What the hell, I got a few minutes. Gotta do what I can to help the kid, right?"

Yeah, he was a real bleeding heart. "You're a good man," I said with a sincerity that equaled his. I wished I'd worn hip boots.

"Shoot," Hunt said.

Don't tempt me, pal.

"What do you want to know?" he asked.

That was why it was probably a good idea to come prepared. I'd have to try that one of these days. Just not today. I'd only gone there to look him over. If the police couldn't break him at the time of Belle Cannon's arrest, I sure wasn't going to get anything from him. My thumbnail screws were in the shop. I could have used Nuri's tape, but I needed to understand what it meant before that would carry any weight. Besides, it was probably smarter to wait until this guy's back was to the wall before I started shoving. Something told me he was far too good at shoving back.

∞

Who was I kidding? There was something I wanted to know, all right. I wanted it so badly, it pushed every other thought from my mind. The tip had come from Tony. I had stopped off at the restaurant again and shared Taylor's belief in Hunt's complicity.

"I tell-a you, Tracy. Taylor, he is right. This man Hunt is barbarian," Tony had said with fierce insistence.

"What do you know about Hunt, Tony?" It sounded like he knew more than he was telling.

Tony's temper flared. "How should I know of such a man?"

That was the problem, I suspected. He knew something, he just didn't want to reveal *how* he knew it. If I couldn't provide him with a plausible reason for it, I was never going to drag it from him.

"Come on, Tony, you serve New York's beautiful people. You must hear gossip."

He picked up a letter-opener and absently cut grooves into his desk. "*Sì*, I hear. But I no like gossip."

"For Marisa . . . ? Is Hunt married?"

Tony shook his head. "No, I never hear that."

"But there are women, right?" If he didn't stop with the letter-opener, I feared he would whittle the Grand Canyon into the desk's surface.

"*Certo!* Certainly. He is a man, no?"

"Young girls?" I suggested eagerly.

"You think-a they would be too young, and you would blackmail Hunt, eh, Tracy?" Tony reasoned with more street smarts than I would have credited him with possessing. "It will-a no work. The woman in his life until recently, she is older."

"You know her?" I demanded.

"You know her, too, Tracy."

"I do?" I asked.

"*Sì*. I hear you talking about her with Charlotte."

My mind went blank. "Who . . . ?"

"Zoya Vrescu."

No way. Zoya was much older than Hunt. The thug couldn't be more than thirty-five. Still, I remembered the look she gave Drew at the airport and the young men with her.

"You've seen them together, Tony?"

"*Sì,* together."

"Here?" I asked.

His defensiveness returned. "Where else am I gonna see them?"

"Maybe they were just talking business," I suggested.

"Maybe was business, but believe-a me, Tracy, was not *all* business. With Zoya, love for Hunt was almost an obsession."

A problem down in the kitchen had taken Tony away, which suited me fine after that bombshell. Even if it was true, I knew there could be any number of logical explanations. Still, I didn't want it to be true.

∞

"Well?" Hunt asked, clearly tired of waiting.

"Is it true you're personally involved with Zoya Vrescu, the dancer?"

We find few enough satisfactions in this life to let any pass without savoring. I would go to my grave with a warm sense of accomplishment for being one of the few people to have ever thrown Lord Hunt out of kilter. He said nothing at first, but a red glow spread up his neck from inside his collar. I didn't think my friend, the deity, liked being on the receiving end of surprises.

"Who told you that?" he demanded.

I shrugged. "It's common knowledge."

"Better not be," he said, his murky eyes issuing a pointed warning. "Zoya and me, we like to keep our business quiet."

"Isn't she a little old for you, Lord?"

Hunt's thin lips twisted into an ugly smile. "Jealous?"

I shot him a look to drive that thought from his tiny mind.

"I like a woman that's been around." Hunt limped to the gun cabinet with the open door. Was he planning to whack me? I held my breath. Fortunately, he just wanted to shut the door. "A broad like that with her connections, she's got class. You know what I mean? I like class."

Obviously why he had so much. "So it's true?"

"Nah, not anymore."

Tony had said the relationship had ended. For a guy who didn't like gossip, Tony was proving to be a good source.

"Who dumped whom? If you don't mind my asking."

Hunt nearly tripped returning to the desk. "What if I do? I thought you were a nice girl, but you don't care what you say."

Girl? We were nearly the same age — had anyone heard me calling him a boy? As far as *nice* went, at least I hadn't shot anyone.

"But what the hell — since you already know. I said I like 'em older, but not *old*. I mean, I'd already got whatever — Besides, she was clinging. What can I say? She had to go."

19

I left Hunt's office in a daze. Zoya had lied to me. Well, failed to tell me the whole truth — same difference. When Hunt's name surfaced, wasn't that her cue to reveal their connection? I was freaking crushed, dammit!

Maybe she was just embarrassed about the dalliance. I would have been. Or that she'd been drop-kicked from it. She certainly hadn't acted like someone harboring a guilty secret. Or like a woman nursing a broken heart, for that matter.

I stopped short with a sudden idea, causing what felt like a football player on Rollerblades to crash into me.

"Why don't you watch where you're going?" the bruiser complained, once he regained his balance.

I shouted a vague apology as he bladed off and pursued my thought in motion. What if Zoya had been the one to break it off? She didn't seem the clingy type, while he did appear to be the kind of man who couldn't admit to being set adrift by a woman he considered lucky to have him. Tony described Zoya's regard for Hunt as obsessive, but Signor Tony Lora clearly had an agenda of his own that I had yet to crack.

I shivered. Not because a can of Play-Doh had been spotted in the vicinity of my idol's feet, I was just cold. During my time with Hunt, dark clouds had moved in, and the wind had picked up. Good-bye, Indian Summer.

It wasn't a surprise. The temperature dipped so low last night, I'd been forced to sleep close to Drew for the warmth. Poor Marisa. Wherever she was, I prayed her captors were keeping her warm and fed. Poor Tony, too — if he was as innocent as I hoped. But that note stuck to his apartment fridge kept nagging at me.

I considered taking the subway back to the house so I could pick up a jacket, but I wasn't eager to run into Drew again. Instead, I called Nuri's dispatcher, then stood over a manhole cover, letting the steam that rises from New York streets warm me till he arrived.

My mind kept returning to Hunt. Why was I fighting it? The last chilling thing he said told the story — people who ceased to serve a purpose had to go.

I probably got it right during the Eaton family's first discussion. Belle Cannon, working for Hunt, snatched Marisa outside the bridal shop. I couldn't say how Belle knew where to find Marisa, but that was the easy part. Her gunning for me with the van made less sense. No one else in the family had been in any jeopardy. Why would Belle assume me to be such a dangerous character I had to be put out of action?

Maybe the close call was an accident. If she had just grabbed Marisa, she'd want to speed away. Perhaps I blocked the street. I tried to recapture that fleeting image, but I feared I'd colored the past too much to trust it.

∾

When Nuri arrived, bright-eyed and eager, I asked him to find me a clothing store. That sucked the wind from his sails.

I'm not much of a shopper, much to my mother's dismay. But Marisa is, and I knew she intended for us to plunder Bloomingdale's and Bergdorf's together this week. The discount store Nuri chose, which smelled of the exhaust from the Burger King next door, would have crushed Marisa, as would my discipline. I just yanked a kelly green acrylic sweater from a sale rack and paid for it without even trying it on.

The clouds had drifted away by the time I left the store. Maybe I'd been a little hasty with the sweater, but if I bought it, I was going to wear it. Nuri had promised to keep circling the block. Knowing New York blocks, however, he could be some time.

Using the sunlit window as a mirror, I pulled the sweater over my head. The reason it was on sale became apparent instantly — chubby little chipmunks were appliquéd across my chest. This sweater probably exceeded even my fashion indifference, but I owned it now. While fixing my fair hair with my fingers, I noticed I wasn't the only person reflected on that window. Through a break in pedestrian traffic, I watched the arrival across the street of someone I planned to visit soon. No question, it was Big-Dan, the large man from the restaurant co-op meeting, who was so eager to sell to Hunt.

With his florid face more flushed than it had been at the meeting, he seemed irritated now. Big-Dan wore a blue blazer and grey slacks that looked good from across the street but a little small for his current weight. He paced within a few feet of the spot where his cab deposited him, shoved his sleeve up to glare at his watch, then resumed his tight pacing. Relief flooded his ruddy face when a cab screeched to a halt. Big-Dan pulled the back door open before the car came to a full stop and reached into the back seat to yank someone out.

Now this *was* interesting. The person racing to meet Big-Dan was none other than Bleached Blondie, Lord Hunt's receptionist. I was sure of it. The features some plastic surgeon had created weren't that memorable, but those silicon boobs were, as well as the condescending expression only the truly stupid seem to capture. Of course, this meeting could be personal. But I had a little trouble cramming a coincidence of that dimension down my delicate throat.

They started walking together. I followed along on my side of the street. I couldn't let those two out of my sight.

If I'd had any doubts about the nature of this get-together, what I saw would have squelched them. Big-Dan never took her hand, and they walked a little apart, the way strangers do when they don't want to touch. This tryst wasn't between Dan and that woman but between him and Hunt.

Nuri cruised past, pausing only to show he understood with a nod. He drove as slowly as possible, given the flow of traffic. I'd just have to leave it to him to coordinate things when he could.

Their stroll soon petered out. They stopped at a

crowded bus stop. But they stood apart from the people waiting for the bus. They faced each other now and kept stealing looks over their shoulders to see whether anyone was watching them from either direction. Neither seemed to give a thought to those of us across the street. Amateurs. She must have stretched out her surveillance too much for him. Finally, he barked something that caused her to shortcut her caution. She shoved her hand into her big Gucci purse — Hunt paid well — and produced an envelope. A nice fat one. What do you bet it didn't contain a letter?

Once the envelope made its appearance, the girl couldn't wait to get rid of it. She thrust it at him, as if it were on fire. His actions were smoother. He eased it from her hand and slipped it into the inner pocket of his navy blazer. Obviously not his first time.

Big-Dan surprised me by sprinting into the slowing traffic and flagging a cab. For a large man, the guy could really move. Nuri was more than a block ahead. When I saw him slowing for a red light, I knew I had a chance. Running faster than I had since high school track, I threw myself into the back seat just as the light turned green.

"Tracy, you scared me!" Nuri complained, clutching his chest.

Scared him? Someday I would shave one of those corners too finely. But not today.

Nuri reversed direction and followed Big-Dan's cab toward downtown. Was he going back to his restaurant?

Suddenly, his cab pulled over, and Dan leaped out. He dashed across the street through a lucky break in traffic and disappeared through the entrance of a hotel. Unable to react as quickly, Nuri dropped me off down the block. I rushed back, not slowing till I passed through the door. I came to a halt once I entered the voluminous lobby. Big-Dan was nowhere in sight.

Wonderful. I couldn't think of any better place to hide than a hotel. If he was visiting someone's room, I was out of luck. It occurred to me that a person with a windfall might be eager to drop some of it. That narrowed the search to the shops and the restaurants. I did a quick sweep through the shopping section and debated between the hotel's better restaurant and its coffee shop. Decisions, decisions. I came down on the side of speed. The coffee shop was busy but not full, and the harried hostess was happy to let me walk through the tables looking for my "friend." Wrong choice.

A small crowd of suits waiting to be seated had gathered outside the better restaurant. I figured I'd pull the same ploy, until I heard the maitre d' say he wouldn't seat anyone until the entire party arrived. I'd have to be more inventive.

"May I see a menu," I asked, after muscling my way to the front of the line. Okay, so it wasn't that inventive.

Being unusually considerate, I rejected the crowded doorway as the place to read the menu and chose a little spot between a waiter's station and the corner. If the host happened to forget about me, all the better. I spread the menu across my face and peered over the top. Pay dirt. Big-Dan was seated at a table almost directly across the room from me. With him was a big, beefy woman with fiery red hair.

Dear God! Belle Cannon? Since her back was to me, I

couldn't see her face. I watched them intently, desperately seeking some giveaway gesture that would establish her identity. The redhead must have eaten alone; the table was set for one, and only scraps of her food remained. A waiter noticed Big-Dan when he brought the check and offered him something, but Dan vigorously shook his head and took the check. He slipped the fat envelope from his pocket and spread it open. It was stuffed with money. Some surprise.

Big-Dan's face tightened when he looked at his watch. He reached into the envelope, pulled out a small fistful of bills, which scarcely diminished their number, and passed them to his companion.

The implications staggered me. Was he a conduit between Hunt and Belle? Hunt shouldn't need a go-between with Belle.

The host attempted to make eye contact with me. He hadn't said anything about my corner spot, but he wanted me to know I was being monitored. Time to move. I'd just hang at the end of the waiting line until Dan and his companion came out. It shouldn't take long. He looked like he was just waiting for change. I returned the menu to the maitre d' with a noncommittal smile and stole another look at Big-Dan's table. Just in time.

They were leaving — but by another exit. I couldn't let them slip away before I saw that woman's face. With my heart racing, I backed into the restaurant, away from the front desk. When the maitre d' answered the phone, I twirled around to run after them. But I crashed into a waiter carrying a tray filled with enough food to feed India for a week, all of which came down on me when I fell.

I struggled to rise. But the tray, the food and the broken dishes were all over me. As well as about a half-dozen people, all speaking at once, asking about everything from the state of my health, to the state of my mind, to whether I had a good lawyer. Try a houseful. I couldn't even push myself up; the floor was covered with broken glass. I would be there still if the maitre d' hadn't taken hold of my arm and yanked me to my feet.

Before he could launch his tirade, I slipped from his grasp and dashed through the door Big-Dan and the redhead had taken. It led to an empty bar. I followed a corridor off the bar all the way to a side door and stuck my head out. They were long gone.

∞

"Tracy, where have you been?" Nuri asked, when I returned to the cab. "What happened? Didn't you just buy that sweater?"

You'd think a married man would know better.

Nuri took off, zipping through traffic without conferring with me. Didn't matter. I needed all my energy to control the queasiness rolling through my stomach from the overpowering stench of the Lobster Newburg wafting off my sweater. I looked at the food-spattered faces of the jolly chipmunks on my chest. At least I'd never have to see the little bastards again.

"I worried when I didn't see you," Nuri said. "He came out long ago."

"You mean Big-Dan came this way? What happened to the woman? He met a big, redheaded woman in there."

Maybe this wasn't dead — yet.

Nuri just shook his head. "She wasn't with him. He waited on the corner; a car came for him."

"Who was driving it, Nuri?"

"I couldn't see anyone behind the wheel at first. Then I discovered the driver was just a small woman."

"His wife." It occurred to me that Nuri's cab was covering a big chunk of Manhattan real estate. "Are we going somewhere?"

"I think I might know where they are headed," Nuri said, his concentration tight.

This was more like it. If we could catch up with Big-Dan, I'd make him lead me to the woman. But what were the odds? I knew how many cars there were in New York City. I'd stuck my head under many of the finer ones, hadn't I? What choice did I have?

Nuri drove with such determination, my energy soared. I channeled it into a search of every car on the road. My focus was so complete, I didn't notice anything — until I saw we were crossing water.

"Nuri, where are we going?" This quest was starting to look hopeless again.

"There they are!" Nuri shouted.

He pointed to a gold Mercedes, well ahead of us but still within reach. A bunch of junk piled in the back seat blocked the head of the driver, but Big-Dan in the passenger seat towered above it. We were closing the gap. Yes! This was the way it was supposed to work.

I couldn't stop laughing. "This is too much even for me. I'll believe in anything now, I swear it. I'll watch tabloid television and swallow every word. I'll buy the Brooklyn Bridge. I'll trust politicians and televangelists. I'll — "

A loud burst, the squeal of tires, and the unmistakable sound of metal against metal arrested my conversion. A car ahead of us suffered a blowout that sent it reeling across the road and started a cataclysmic chain of events that touched each of the thousands of people behind it. The good news was that Nuri's cab wasn't one of the cars that crashed. You can guess the bad news.

I didn't say anything for a while. Finally, I asked, "Where were they headed?"

Nuri sighed. "The airport."

I grasped at the smallest of straws. "Maybe they were only going to pick someone up, and they'll be at their restaurant the same as always tonight."

"Tracy, I didn't merely guess at their destination. I had a reason for thinking they would drive this way," Nuri said with a blend of compassion and exasperation. "The back seat of the Mercedes was filled with luggage."

The junk. Of course it was.

What if I wasn't lucky *or* good?

20

My mood, when Nuri dropped me off in the alley behind The Gypsy Princess, was sour. I pitied anyone who got in my way. Poor Tony.

While I suffered through the eternity it took for the police to break up that nightmare traffic jam on the bridge, I had a great many thoughts. None of them printable. I told myself it wasn't a disaster that Big-Dan had slipped away. That the redhead didn't have to be Belle Cannon. That there might be a simple explanation for Dan's involvement with Hunt. I told myself a lot of things. I didn't buy any of them. Alternative theories were possible, however.

The redhead really *didn't* have to be Belle. The musculature I saw straining against the tight cotton dress of the woman Big-Dan met looked too young to belong to someone Belle's age. Who else could she have been? Try Dan's daughter. Was it so farfetched to imagine a small redheaded woman and a big man producing a large red-haired child? Even if the little wife died her hair blonde now, her freckles told me she was born with red hair. Not all heavily freckled faces were redheads, but many of them were. Would it be so surprising if the offspring of those two also had money problems and wanted her cut when Mom and Dad enjoyed a windfall?

If that theory was right, Big-Dan probably had nothing to do with the kidnapping. Hunt would have paid him to spy on his fellow co-op members and lobby them to sell. Dan and his wife were probably just skipping out on their debts.

The worst of it was not having any way to uncover the truth. No, the very worst was being beaten by a man who hadn't even known I was in hot pursuit. Pride could be so cruel.

∞

I fished the elevator key Tony had given me from my backpack. That elevator was a pretty basic affair that always seemed to smell strongly of vegetables. It also lacked the insulation of passenger elevators. Sounds from the busy kitchen above echoed in its shaft, grating against my already raw nerves.

I slipped into the kitchen and stood off to the side, watching the bustling activity. Tony was displaying the preparation of a dish to a pair of cooks, but his pace seemed a beat too slow. His heart wasn't in it. I wondered how he explained Marisa's absence. He probably gave some ridiculous wedding excuse that not even the most naive among them believed. They had to think Tony and Marisa had split up. If I didn't watch myself, I'd start feeling too sorry for him to carry out my plan.

Tony took advantage of my appearance to leave his attempt at carrying on, and we went into his small office.

He was so distracted, he never even commented on the food-spattered rodents on my sweater.

"Tracy, you have learned something new?" he asked in his heavy accent.

I gave my head a grave shake; on the basis of that refrigerator note, I'd acted on a hunch. I was prepared for this encounter.

"*Dio mio!*"

"You know, Tony, when you're under all this stress, you shouldn't add to the pressure by forcing yourself to speak in Italian."

"I no understand you, Tracy." His eyes didn't meet mine.

Though that little room would feel claustrophobic with the door closed, I shut it and stood with my back pressed against it. No one was leaving till I had my say.

"Game's over, pal. I called your Italian cooking school. Guess what? They have no record of anyone named Tony Lora ever attending."

I slipped a piece of paper from my pocket and slapped it before him on the desk. It was the note he'd written to Marisa, which I took from their apartment. He stared at it, his head bent, his body still. Maybe he was trying to invent a plausible reason why a man who could barely speak the language would write in apple pie American English.

I waited through the heavy silence, but when his eyes failed to move from the note, I went on. "That's right, they've never had an Italian student named Tony Lora. But get this. There was an American in Marisa's class who fit your description — and his name was John Anthony Briachi."

"Junior," Tony snapped in perfect English. "That changes everything."

I didn't know about it changing everything. It meant he wasn't the same John Anthony Briachi about to stand trial, but it put him a little too close for comfort.

He absently pressed down the curling corner of a travel poster hanging near him. "My name really is Tony. I've always used my middle name. And Lora was my mother's maiden name."

"Why the change?"

"Get real, Tracy. If your father was one of history's most notorious crime bosses, would you want to carry his name? I have nothing to do with his business or with the family."

He didn't mean the family, he meant The Family. I distinctly heard the caps.

"People change their names all the time without assuming a role. Incidentally, that was the worst Italian accent I've ever heard."

Tony looked surprised. "Really? I was trying to mimic the way my grandfather used to speak, but he's been dead for years."

Given that family's connections, I didn't ask how he died.

"Talking like that was a joke that got away from us. When Marisa and I started dating, neither of us intended to get serious. She didn't want a relationship that would interfere with her career, and I wouldn't inflict the burden of my family on anyone." Tony's sigh sounded old and bitter. "We were still trying to keep it light when Marisa's parents came to visit. We knew they wouldn't be happy

about her dating a mobster's son. Since I'd already decided to begin using my mother's name when I returned
to the States, I just started it a little early."

"That still doesn't explain the accent." Even though
I'd found that accent suspicious for a while, his normal
speech made him seem like a different man. One I didn't
know.

"Marisa said her father was a sharp lawyer. I had this
bright idea an accent would complete my disguise. I didn't
know we were going to fall in love. I sure as hell wouldn't
have started it if I was going to be stuck with it for life.
Can you imagine what would happen should they find out
who I really am?"

"You're underestimating Taylor, Tony. I'm sure he
knows."

Tony snorted in disbelief.

"He wouldn't let some stranger walk off with his only
daughter without doing a little checking. All it took me
was a phone call. As a sneak, you're not very good."

"I take that as a compliment." He removed his white
chef's hat and ran his fingers through his soft hair. "Do
you think Charlotte knows?"

"I don't know. Has she given birth to any barnyard
animals lately?"

Tony laughed, and I realized it was the first happy
sound I'd heard him make. It didn't last.

"You're just lucky you came along after my marriage
to Drew softened her up, or she wouldn't accept even Tony
Lora."

He nodded absently, no longer laughing. "Now you
can see why I didn't want the police involved."

"No, Tony, I can't." I took the chair across from Tony's desk, an ancient, black vinyl secretarial chair with busted springs.

"I couldn't risk someone leaking it. Can you imagine the field day the press would have? If it got out, Marisa would be in even greater danger."

"How?" I asked.

Tony formed his hands into such tight fists, his knuckles went white. "I'm sure Hunt is behind this. Who else would be? But he isn't doing the job himself. What do you think small-time thugs would do with the 'evidence' when they found they were holding John Anthony Briachi's future daughter-in-law? Marisa wouldn't see another day."

That was a wrinkle I hadn't considered. It wasn't just Tony's way of speaking that had changed; he suddenly seemed a more worldly man.

The chair's lack of springs allowed me to fall into a thoughtful rocking. "You know, Tony, I saw him once watching The Princess. Your father, I mean."

"I've seen him, too. I just never acknowledge it."

There was a small window on the outside wall, too high for most people to look out. Below it on the floor, I noticed a little white plastic stool jammed between the cases stacked against the wall.

"He's giving me another chance to admit I made a mistake by not following in his footsteps. On the eve of his trial, he still doesn't have any regrets!" Tony shook his head in bitter frustration. "I haven't spoken to him or visited his house in over two years, and I never will again."

I drummed my fingertips against the front of the desk, hesitating before proceeding. "Tony, there's another possibility here. We've discussed the revenge idea, that some-one has it in for Hunt. Maybe Hunt is just a convenient object. The revenge could be aimed at — "

"Me? You think my father has staged this kidnapping to get back at me? Tracy, you don't know what you're talking about. I'm his son, his flesh. No matter what has happened between us, he would never do this to me. How could you think it?"

It was something we both thought. I was just the only one who'd admit it. I stepped onto the stool and pushed open the window. It was the perfect height to look out.

Tony buried his face in his arms. I thought he was about to cry, but he lifted his head and merely rubbed his tired, old eyes.

"You aren't going to tell Drew about me, are you, Tracy? I'm not sure he would understand. There's a lot of Charlotte in him."

Tell me about it. I promised Tony I wouldn't tell anyone.

"I'm glad you know, Tracy. You can't imagine how isolated I've felt."

Working alone to find Marisa, I bet I could.

"Marisa and I were going to let the accent dissolve over the next couple of years, but in the meantime it was our private joke. Now it's become an albatross. And the truth about my identity — well, I told you why I have to keep that quiet. Marisa's life depends on it. But it's frustrating; I haven't been able to tell anyone what I know, even if it might help. That's why I told you I saw Hunt and Zoya *here*."

I jumped from the stool. "Excuse me?"

"Lord Hunt and Zoya Vrescu — remember, I said they used to be a couple? I told you I saw them together here."

"Then — where did you see them?"

"My parents' house. Hunt used to bring her there. My father and Hunt do business together."

21

Let me see if I had this straight. Marisa was kidnapped by someone who might have been operating either with or without the knowledge of Mr. Godlike Hunt, but who was undoubtedly working for his benefit. Mr. Hunt, who may or may not have been involved with my idol, the great Zoya Vrescu. Mr. Hunt, who might have some business dealings with the infamous Mr. In-Big-Trouble Briachi, Sr., who could have engineered this whole event to get back at his son for rejecting his life's work, even though he was the intended father-in-law of the victim. The victim, who was the niece of the man, himself missing, who may or may not have been known to the great Zoya Vrescu, and who may or may not have been planning to snare the Godlike-one in one of his scams. Did I have it straight? Of course not! I didn't even write them this complicated.

I was so lost in that maze when I left Tony, I didn't notice that the man I bumped into just outside the doorway was none other than my own, currently less-than-dear husband. He didn't bat an eye about my food-soaked sweater. Something told me the honeymoon was dead and buried.

"Long time no see," Drew said.

I wondered what the Weavers would make of his verbal efforts.

"What are you doing here, Drew?" I blocked the doorway to the building's lobby with my arm.

"Just thought I'd see how Tony was holding up."

"He's not doing too well, but I think he wants to be alone." Tony couldn't handle Drew just now.

Drew nodded his understanding, and we fell into walking together. Neither of us talked at first, but it wasn't one of the comfortable silences we used to share.

Finally, I asked, "How's it coming, Drew?"

"Not good." He hesitated before the truth poured out. "I think Philly lied about this guy who bought his share. I'm not sure he really exists."

No flies on him. Viciously, I kicked a soda can lying on the sidewalk. "Drew, what's the deal with Philly?"

He stiffened defensively. "I don't know what you mean."

"Honey, cut the crap."

"How do I explain Philly?" Drew's approach sounded as if he were addressing one of life's eternal mysteries. "He's a free spirit, a man-child. He's an entrepreneur with — unusual standards."

"He's a con artist." Gave the can a little tap.

Drew sighed in surrender. "Right. How did you know?"

"Remember that day you *weren't* following him? Well, *if* you had followed him, it would have been a good thing *if* he had shaken you — the police picked up anyone who even looked twice at him."

Drew stared at me, his golden eyes wide. "You were picked up by the police?"

"Sure was." I gave the can another kick, harder this time.

He muttered an apology. "Was it awful?"

"It wasn't the way I intended to spend my vacation." It was better, but let him think I suffered. "Drew, why does everyone lie about Philly?"

Drew sped up and reached the spot where the can landed before I did. Ever responsible, he tossed it into a trash container. "To call it lying is an exaggeration, Tracy, but you can see how Philly manages to upset everything. If Marisa — "

I hate when people steal my toys. "This has nothing to do with Marisa. The lies date back before she was taken. It was ages after we were married before you told me your mother had a brother. You wouldn't answer my questions about him. Sure, I can see how Philly would embarrass your family, but you had to know he wouldn't bother me. What's the big secret?"

It exploded from him. "I don't know!"

I waited.

At last, he said, "There's always been some secret between my parents and Philly — since that year in Europe. Before that Philly wasn't really welcome in our house. Mom would have a cow when he came. She was always trying to turn Corbett and me against him. It wasn't fair — we loved them both. But even as kids, we knew what Philly was."

He thought he could hide it from me. What did that say about his opinion of my intelligence?

"After they came home from Europe, everything

changed," Drew admitted. "Philly would show up more regularly, and my parents tried to make him feel welcome, though you could see it killed them. Philly acted like he belonged there, as if he had a right to us kids. It was almost as if, as if — " Drew tripped over the words. " — he was blackmailing them!"

"Some leap, Drew. What do you think is behind it?"

"Maybe my father let himself be roped into one of Philly's deals. I can't think of anything else." He shrugged and stuck his hands into his pockets. Despite his smart black polo shirt and jeans so rigidly creased they could walk without him — with his shoulders hunched over, he looked a sorry sight. "I don't know, and I don't want to know, Tracy. I *never* want to know."

We passed a newspaper stand; Tony's father's exploits dominated the headlines again. "Secrets usually come out eventually."

"Not if everyone leaves them alone. The rest of them will — you're the only danger." He came to a halt and took my arm. "Promise me, Tracy, *please* promise me, you won't look into it?"

You'd think he'd have learned by now. I'd promise him anything. "Andrew, can't you accept that your parents are human, that they've made mistakes?" He never had any trouble believing it of me.

"No, I can't. I won't."

I shouted in exasperation, "You're an adult!"

He stopped short of denying it. "You know, Tracy, the widely held belief that you can never go home is wrong. The trouble is, you can."

22

After warning me away from the covert part of his family's history, Drew announced he had to be alone and went off on his own. Fine with me. I needed time to roll that little blackmail gem around in my mind. I slipped into a bar where I could do it in comfort.

I took a table in the rear where stray conversations wouldn't intrude on my thoughts. Not that there would be many. There were only a couple of guys seated at the bar, but it still took forever before the bartender condescended to take my order. Sauvignon Blanc is my usual drink, but as the air was nippy today, I ordered red wine.

"We only have California," the bartender said.

This guy was asking for it. As if that weren't enough, he couldn't keep his eyes off the buffet on my sweater.

"You got a problem?" I snapped. I'd been there too long. I was starting to sound brusque enough to be a native.

No question, New Yorkers were a strange bunch, at least to my California eyes. Once I saw a man in full Viking regalia standing at attention on a crowded New York street corner. Would you believe — I was the only person who found him interesting enough to stop for a chat. I won't lie, their eccentricities were wearing thin.

I sipped my Napa Valley nectar, hoping it would restore my spirits. I couldn't give in to the fatigue and confusion I felt. Time was running out.

I batted around Drew's belief that Taylor had slipped from the path of sunlight into Philly's dark clutches. I didn't buy it. Taylor was too shrewd to be taken in by someone like Philly, and if he had, he was too savvy not to fix it. But it didn't surprise me Drew believed it. The fear born in his childhood had been preserved in the murkiest corner of his mind. If he studied it now through adult eyes, he'd see that Taylor didn't fit the part. But he wouldn't like the alternative casting any better.

If I were picking guilty parties, Charlotte would be my choice. Not only did she lack Taylor's business sense, I'd noticed that, despite what siblings might think about each other, they shared unbreakable bonds. If Philly were in trouble, I could see Charlotte taking foolhardy risks to save him. The question was: To what lengths would she go to hide them now? Appearance mattered to her. So much that she'd sacrifice her daughter to preserve them?

No, that was unthinkable. She was Marisa's mother, for chrissakes. Still, Charlotte and Taylor were hiding something. Even if it was ancient history, it had a bearing on our present dilemma.

But which of them wasn't hiding something? I found myself doubting them all. Was I really sure that had been Corbett's voice I heard when I rang that number in Paris? And how about Charlotte? When I searched Marisa's apartment, I'd joked to myself that it looked like Charlotte had cleaned it. Maybe she did. How could I say she hadn't gone there and covered critical evidence of Marisa's disappearance? As for Taylor — well, I'd always thought there might be another side to him, behind the patrician good looks and the bonhomie he showed the family. What did I really know about the man who rose to considerable heights on Wall Street? Tony was still a wild card. And Zoya? How did she keep her stories straight?

They all farmed a hidden patch overgrown with guilty little secrets. Perhaps it was time to weed one of them. Since I'd lectured Drew on the necessity of interacting with his parents as an adult, it was essential that I not behave like anyone's five-year-old fan. I downed my drink and shot out of there before I could change my mind.

⟨∞⟩

Zoya welcomed me into her humbling abode with open arms and a show of earnest concern. Once again, she didn't comment on my appearance. She probably believed I was a natural pig. Who cared? I thought I would need to strengthen my resolve, but anger did it for me, though whether I was angry with her for lying or at myself for swallowing her lies, I couldn't say.

"Tracy, come in. Has there been any news about . . . " She seemed to search for the name. " . . . Marisa?"

She led me into the lush sitting room and indicated one of her prissy little chairs, while she arranged herself on the velvet sofa.

"None, I'm afraid. I feel so helpless," I said.

"I also wish I could save that poor child from suffering. But what could I do?"

Talk about setups. "Well, Zoya, you could start by asking your ex-boyfriend to return Marisa."

The jowly maid came in, as she was doubtless ordered to do when guests visited. Zoya froze her with a look that made the woman back out.

"I — I don't understand," Zoya sputtered.

"You can't have forgotten that you and Hunt were an item."

"Who told you that?" she asked.

"He did."

Zoya hesitated, then shrugged. "I know what you're thinking, Tracy. If I lied about one thing, I might be lying about other things as well, but I'm not. Surely you can understand it was too awkward to mention."

I hammered on with frank persistence. "Who dumped whom?"

Zoya spread her fingers on the armrest and examined her scarlet nails. "Dumped — such an ugly word. You must learn those tough words from writing your books."

If she thought the Tessa Graham Mysteries were hard-boiled, she was reading the wrong books.

She rose and walked to the baby grand piano, which she leaned on as she gazed out the window. "If you must know, Tracy, I ended it. It was never very serious on my side, though it was a good mutual exchange while it lasted. I gave him some polish — you've seen how badly he needs it. And he helped me to make some good real estate deals. But he was becoming too possessive. He didn't take it well when I told him it was over."

From the smile she gave me, you'd think we were engaging in girl-talk, just trashing the boys. I saw none of the obsessive love Tony described.

"To tell you the truth, Tracy, when you mentioned Hunt the first time, I'd almost forgotten I knew him." She fussed with the spray of yellow flowers in a crystal vase on the baby grand.

"I'm sure you've known many men, Zoya."

"My, yes," she said with a silvery laugh.

"And forgotten a number of them?"

"Of course." She tilted her head to study the adjustment she'd made to the flowers.

"Perhaps that's the case with Philly Chase," I suggested.

"Philly? Oh, that funny little man. My taste is eclectic, but it has never run to anything that seedy. Believe me, Tracy, if he had been in my life, I would have remembered."

I believed her. Why shouldn't I? That next to me on the end table rested an old Meerschaum pipe filled with a still-warm plug of Philly's favorite tobacco didn't mean anything. Many men smoked Flying Dutchman. The question was: Did Zoya's taste run to any of them?

∞

Before I left Zoya's apartment, I returned to the subject of Hunt and introduced his involvement with Briachi. Zoya dragged herself back to the sofa with poor grace, swearing all the while that she'd never met Briachi and certainly hadn't visited his home.

"To think I would know such a pretentious lowlife. Really, Tracy. What kind of person do you think I am?"

She was less adamant about the former recipient of

her polish, but suggested there was no basis for any involvement between them. Her manner was as smooth as ever, yet the tension tightened her face enough to knock off a few years. Was she protecting her ex-lover or herself? How clean were some of those deals Hunt put together for her?

I didn't think Tony was lying about Hunt's involvement with Briachi, although he hadn't done much to enhance his credibility lately. The trouble was I hadn't questioned him thoroughly enough, and Zoya nailed me in one of my weak spots.

"What business could they have together?" she asked.

I hadn't a clue. Drug distribution seemed a big part of Briachi's operation, so I suggested that. Talk about standing on quicksand.

"Drugs? How absurd you are, Tracy." She adjusted the folds of her full white skirt till it looked pleated. "No one with as high a profile as Lord Hunt could possibly pull it off."

"That's precisely why no one would suspect it. He has too much money, and it came too fast."

"Bah! You know nothing!" Zoya insisted, her accent of origin growing unaccountably heavier.

She hadn't danced this fast when I saw her on stage. Still, I couldn't hammer all the nails into the coffin. Before I took my departure, she encouraged me to keep at it, exaggerating my prowess as a detective even more than I did. If she were involved, she would hardly set the dogs on herself.

This time, I didn't float from the apartment on her praise. It simply didn't mean that much to me. My regard for her had diminished irrevocably. But I'd left there with a dent in my usually impregnable armor of confidence, as well. I'd been so pleased with myself for blowing Tony's cover, I hadn't pressed him hard enough. I didn't know what I needed to question her effectively.

That could be fixed. I hightailed it back to The Gypsy Princess and slipped into the alley. It was a good thing I happened to be walking close the building. The driver of the limousine that tore up the center of the alley would never have seen me in the shadows and, at that speed, would not have been able to stop. Arrogant bastard. Some people don't care about anyone else. I'd noticed that living within the confines of that urban tunnel were several families of cats.

I assumed the limo driver was using the alley as a shortcut, but the car stopped about halfway along. All the rear entrances tended to look alike. But I would swear on oath that the limousine was parked behind The Gypsy Princess, though admittedly, that meant less to me than it was supposed to.

I needed a closer look, but too many Dumpsters blocked the way. I crept up to a Dumpster a couple of doors away from The Princess and quickly scaled its side panel, hoping the driver beyond the blackened windows of the limousine wasn't watching my performance in his rearview mirror. I lowered the lid quietly and held it up a few inches with the top of my head. With all that food spattered on my clothes, I should have felt right at home. But it was worse than I imagined. The stench gagged me, my neck developed a spasm from the weight of the lid, and something told me the furry creatures brushing against my legs weren't cats! How could something as politically correct as biodegradability feel so gross? Reality was over-rated.

Making it worse, the bastard behind the wheel took his time about doing anything. Eventually, the car's horn wailed loud and long. A few minutes later, Tony stormed from restaurant's elevator and banged on the driver's window.

Was it my imagination, or was Tony undergoing a subtle transformation? He'd exchanged his kitchen whites for a black silk shirt and black jeans. Decked out well enough for the Saturday night club scene. He'd even slicked back his soft hair with gel. *Nouveau* Mafia look?

The limo driver's window slid down. Tony had words with the person beyond it. Too bad they were all in Italian. Tony returned to the elevator and waited petulantly. After a moment, a large male person in an olive green suit with the bromidic underarm bulge emerged from the car to be followed by a scrawny guy who must've been driving. They followed Tony inside The Princess.

I kept repeating the car's license plate number to my-self. As if there were any question about its ownership. Still, I'm nothing if not thorough — most of the time. Once the elevator doors sealed shut, I scrambled from the Dumpster and rushed to the pay phone on the corner and dialed Weaver's number.

"Give me Detective Weaver. This is an emergency." I must have waited for a week before shouting, "Patch me through."

"What patch?" that familiar magnolia voice demanded. "I'm here at my desk."

"Detective, I need a favor — badly. I want you to run a plate for me." A panhandler with an extended hand brushed close to me. He left when I told him I'd need a buck to complete my call. The hell with American Express, I was never again leaving home without my cell phone.

"Ms. Eaton, I don't work for you, I work for the people of New York. But I couldn't do what you're asking — "

"Look, Weaver, it's in your best interest to do this. I'm working on something really big, and I intend to plop the whole thing in your lap soon, just so you can use it to get back to Manhattan South Homicide."

"Homicide will just have to do without me, I expect," he drawled. "I can't do it — unless you can give me a powerful reason why I should."

"Reason, shmeason," I snapped. "A fan of Tessa Graham's would do it without one!"

Silence. He sighed. "What's the number?"

Jeez, I was only kidding. Was he afraid I was going to tell someone? I rattled off the license plate in the same singsong manner I'd used to keep it in my head.

He wasn't gone long. "Now this is just a onetime favor, Ms. Eaton."

Yeah, yeah — get on with it.

"The car is registered to a company called Quality Imports. Not being a local person, you might not know who's associated with that company."

"Let me guess. John Anthony Briachi."

"On the money," Weaver said. "Now, Ms. Eaton, since I did you this little favor, why don't you come in right now? We can have a lil' chat about what all you think you're doing — "

"Sorry, Detective, I can't do that."

"Ms. Eaton — Tracy, you hear me? I must insist — "

I hung up before he could complete the threat. When they start getting pushy, I'm out of there.

I rushed back to the alley, certain the limo would be gone by now. But it wasn't. I crept to the elevator and opened it with my key. Amidst the chatter echoing in the shaft, one voice stood out.

"Tony, I don't take no orders from you. You wasn't ready to go when I was, so now you'll wait till I'm done eating."

Tony shouted something in Italian, but it sounded like impotent bravado.

Maybe my luck was returning. About time. I closed the elevator doors and glanced at the car. The lazy driver had left the window down. I looked at the trunk. I felt a smile starting on my lips. Should I? Like there was any question.

Reaching into the car, I flipped the trunk latch. Then I raced to the back of the car and crawled into it. Who knew the trunk of a limo would be so big? I'd had smaller apartments. I could stay in there for a long time. Did, too. It must have been fifteen minutes before I heard the elevator doors opening again. The car rocked as three people climbed into it, first in the front, then the rear. I took a firm grip on the trunk latch. I didn't want to get trapped in a locked trunk!

After the car began moving, I had an awful attack of the giggles and had to bite the insides of my cheeks to control it. I kept thinking about that scene in *Goodfellas* when the stiff in the trunk started making all that noise and startled the guys driving the car. I felt an impulse to bang my body around and scare the bejeezus out of those up front — until I remembered how the folks in the movie dealt with that not-quite-dead corpse.

Perhaps I should turn my attention to more serious concerns. I didn't need subtitles to know where we were headed. The prodigal was enjoying a homecoming. And probably not the first, I realized belatedly. Where else would he have learned about Hunt and Zoya's recent breakup, except the only place where he'd seen them together?

23

Parents: Necessary evils or burdens for life?

Think I was being too hard on them? Look at Tony's father and say that. But I'm getting ahead of myself.

The ride in the rear compartment of the limo wasn't bad. We hit a few potholes, but the car had great suspension. I tried memorizing turns and timing distances, but I just became too confused. At best, I concluded we hadn't left New York State. We hadn't driven far enough to reach Connecticut, and my lungs would have told me if we'd used any tunnels. That narrowed the field in case I ever wanted to find my way back.

After clearing an electric gate and coasting down a long driveway, the car finally slowed to a stop. I felt the movement when my fellow passengers slammed their doors shut and heard the crunch of gravel as they walked away. When quiet returned, I slowly raised the trunk. Once my eyes adjusted to the light, I saw we were parked before a large, but not ostentatious, fieldstone manor house. How nice — a hoodlum with taste.

The sight of the immaculately manicured grounds gave me hope. I had been afraid Briachi would use guard dogs.

During the ride, I had checked my backpack for food I could use to distract them, but apart from two fossilized Certs, I came up empty-handed. Fortunately, the carefully maintained lawns reduced the odds of dogs. That daredevil, Briachi. It looked like he was willing to leave his security to nothing more than mere chance, electric gates, barbed wire and an army of thugs.

With thugs in mind, it occurred to me it might be better if I didn't keep making like a statue on the front lawn. I slipped around the side and peeked through first a set of French doors, then a few other windows. All the rooms were unoccupied. They weren't empty showrooms, however; all showed recent evidence of use. They were also decorated in excellent taste. Zoya's place looked downright splashy compared to this.

I'd grown so accustomed to empty rooms, I became a little careless. When I pressed my face to another window along the rear of the house, I noticed this room was occupied. Seated before a television set was a small, middle-aged woman. I figured she was watching the TV, till I saw the screen was black. Her face must have been the saddest I'd ever seen. It looked as if it had been frozen in the moment before the flow of tears, when all hope seemed lost. It didn't feel right to watch her, even to me, nosy as I am. No one showed this face to the world. Doing the only thing I could for her, I crept away from the window and left her alone with her pain.

Both the kitchen and the service porch were empty, but the doors were locked. These weren't trusting people. I remembered passing a trellis of ivy that climbed to the second floor and figured that would be my only way in.

It proved to be an easy climb. My sneakers fit right into the trellis openings, and the old vine kept it steady. I jumped off onto a terrace that skirted part of the second floor. Sidling up to a window, I snatched a glimpse at an empty corridor. Best yet, I'd found an unlocked window. Now we were cooking. There were bound to be keyholes ripe for peeking there. I slipped the window up and crawled through.

Kids, don't try this at home. There's a lesson to be learned here: Looking both ways applies equally to crossing streets and second story work. I'd established the corridor was empty in one direction but ran smack into a welcoming committee when I turned the other way. Well, a committee of one, but he was big.

The manor bouncer's neck must have been as thick as a tree trunk, and the muscles of his mammoth arms rippled beneath the surface of his pearl grey sharkskin suit. He twisted my arms behind my back and pushed me down the hall.

"What gave me away?" I needed to know.

"Motion sensors," was his succinct response.

"*Outdoors?* How do you stop the birds from moving?"

"We stop them."

I bet they did.

He opened a door and threw me into an office. The King of Crime himself sat behind a desk that wasn't one bit bigger than an aircraft carrier. Funny thing though, there were none of the usual guest chairs around it. People stood before this man. Or knelt.

In person, the resemblance between him and Tony was stronger than I'd noticed from the old man's photograph.

But what a variation on the theme. In contrast to Tony's warm, liquid eyes, Briachi's looked like dark, dead sink-holes to hell. His expression was so cold, I figured he could flash-freeze a person with a look. How could a child of this man not be twisted?

"I found *this* crawling through the hall window," the bouncer said, shoving me toward the desk. "Which paper do you think this one writes for?"

So the reporters had been storming the house. Natu-rally, they'd increased surveillance. Was it any wonder I got caught?

Briachi kept his eyes trained on me, while addressing the henchman. "She isn't a reporter. She's the sister-in-law, the one from the Coast."

The? Nice to know he shared my egomaniacal delu-sions.

"Get rid of her," Briachi said.

How did he mean that?

The thug reached for my arm, but I pulled away. "Hold it. I went through a lot to get here, and I'm not ready to leave yet."

I never saw so much as an eyelash flutter from Bria-chi, but permission to speak was apparently granted; the thug backed off. These tough guys sure like their little games.

Since they hadn't provided me with a chair, I had to make my own comfort. I pressed my hands on the glossy surface of the desk and leaned across, until I was less than a foot away from spitting in his eye. Still, I doubted I'd been granted much time. I cut right to it.

"If you're not involved in it, keep out. You'll only get

her killed." As Tony had been there, I felt certain Briachi knew what I meant. I feared he had always known. "If you have her, let her go unharmed and maybe he'll forgive you. Your son — "

For the first time, he spoke directly to me. "I have no son."

Parents: Necessary evils *and* burdens for life. This man knew all of Tony's future in-laws by sight. He risked his life just to gaze at the restaurant. He had to care. But he wouldn't budge the little it would have taken to establish some relationship with his son because that wouldn't have been on Briachi's terms.

"Get her out of here," Briachi said.

"How, boss?" the thug asked. "Stan used the limo to take — " He stopped; the mere mention of Tony's name appeared verboten now. "I mean, he took the limo back to the city."

"Use the Crown Vic. Drive her to the nearest train station and buy her a ticket. And, Sal, explain to her why she should never come back."

I took one last look at Briachi's frigid face before Sal-the-thug dragged me out. I hoped Tony was right about his father not being involved in Marisa's kidnapping. If he was, she didn't have a chance.

∞

The trip back to Manhattan was painful. Sal discovered I wrote the Tessa Graham Mysteries and just couldn't pass up the opportunity to critique them.

"She tawks too good. I don't know no one who tawks

that good."

Could have fooled me.

He also took his orders literally. We could have driven all the way to town in relative comfort, but no, he had to park the car near a station and ride the train with me. On the plus side, no one even considered mugging me.

∞

Once we parted, I hurried to the house with the hope of finding Drew. The last time I saw him, he said he needed to take a long walk alone. By now, he could have run a couple of solitary marathons. I hoped his confusion had cleared enough for some serious talking. There were things I needed to know.

The townhouse didn't reek so strongly of cleaning products now. Charlotte must have discovered some other diversion to channel her nerves. Drew didn't seem to be around, however. I checked the house and was about to escape back to the suite when Charlotte nailed me.

"Tracy, is that you?" she called from the living room. "Come in here, sweetheart, and have a drink."

What fun.

While stalling long enough to disguise the value I placed on her invitation, I noticed the Chinese vase they kept on the foyer Japanese table, and was instantly submerged in a wave of *deja vu*.

My last encounter with that vase happened during my first visit to the Eaton home after our marriage. I returned to the house unexpectedly and heard Drew and his mother talking in the other room.

∞

"But she's so shallow, Drew," Charlotte had said.

"Tracy? You're wrong, Mom. Though I'll grant you she goes to great lengths to create that impression."

They were talking about me! Talk about sticky situations. I knew if I crept from the house and they heard me, they'd consider me a sneak. But if I stayed and they discovered me — they'd *know* I was. My best choice would have been to clear my throat, enter the room, and pretend I never heard a word. Charlotte would be mortified, but that was better than waiting until she said something really awful.

I took a deep breath, vowing to march in there and show her which of us really had the most class — but I didn't move. The truth was I wanted to hear what they had to say.

"What you have to understand is the Graingers are living their lives in a Noel Coward play," Drew said. "They don't know there's a real world out here."

I can't remember for sure, but I think my truly refined mother-in-law snorted at that point. "Son, I think you just proved my point."

She went on to provide a chapter-and-verse account of every time Mother and I strayed from the path of conformity from the instant she'd met us. Who knew she was taking notes?

"They can be trying at times," Drew admitted. "But I'll tell you this, Mom, Tracy and her parents have forgotten more about enjoying life than we ever knew."

My eyes misted. Drew never said that to me; he always focused on the trying-part. I wanted to go in there and plant a big wet one right on his kisser.

Unfortunately, I forgot about my predicament, which was worse now that I'd listened to the entire conversation. Instead of devising a way out of that mess, I fantasized about what I would do to my new husband now that I knew he held me in such awe. While daydreaming, I bumped into the table and started the vase rocking. I tried to catch it — the damn thing was probably Ming! — but that only made it worse.

No, it didn't break. I almost wished it had. Then they would have hated me for being a destructive person, instead of focusing on the truth — that I was a sneaky one. Not to mention shallow. When Drew and his mother rushed into the foyer to save the vase and saw me there, I experienced enough embarrassment to fill twenty lifetimes. No sense of the real world, huh? The look of triumphant scorn I saw on Charlotte's face was branded to my retinas.

I still hated that vase.

∞

"Tracy, what's keeping you?" a peevish Charlotte asked.

I gave the lousy table a wide berth and slowed my walk, unsure whether the face I'd encounter in that room would reflect a memory of that day, too.

I needn't have worried.

Charlotte said, "Make yourself a drink, honey."

She had started without me. That's not to say she was drunk, but let's put it this way: If I decided to practice acupuncture on her, she wouldn't have noticed. For my purposes, her condition was all to the good. Like this, she was more pliable than Drew. Since he could return at any time, I plunged in on the questioning.

"Charlotte, we really have to talk about Philly." I tried to stay focused, but the sight of a glass sweating without a coaster between it and Charlotte's mahogany table proved overwhelming.

"Oh, pooh on Philly! He's always making trouble for me. I'm glad he's gone."

Her statement didn't shock me, just that she ended it with a spitty Bronx cheer.

"I never could count on him except to screw up. Our mother was just as bad. Do you know what it's like growing up with people who'll do *anything*?"

How could she ask? She knew my parents.

"Married, divorced, married, divorced. We never knew who our 'father' would be this week, but it was always just a matter of time until they caught on that Mother was just a cheap gold-digger and booted us out."

Her description didn't jibe with Drew's rendition of his late grandmother.

She thrust her glass at me, sending a spray of condensation onto a sweater that had already seen enough action. "Run to the den and make me a refill, will you, honey? Scotch."

Stunned, I did.

Charlotte began her recitation again on my return. "We never knew what would happen tomorrow. One day we'd be rich and living in a mansion, and the next we'd have to dodge the landlord when she spent her settlement and couldn't pay the rent. She'd throw a party for a thousand people, and the next morning we wouldn't have anything to eat. I know people think I'm too stiff, but I don't care. When you follow the rules, everything's just — safer."

I tried not to show much sympathy; I knew when she was sober she wouldn't want that. What she said, and what she didn't say, broke my heart. I understood her and Philly now. Their mother placed them on a roller coaster and told them that was real life. Philly believed it and never got off, while Charlotte was still trying to make it stop. I had to hand it to those two lovable loonies who raised me. They did an okay job. Sure, they turned me out a trifle out-of-sync with the rest of humanity, but I'd never been in the company of the demons which were probably always with Charlotte. I understood her great need for control and hoped I'd be more generous in the future, even when she didn't seem to deserve it.

The phone rang, and I ran to answer it. "It's someone named Julie," I reported. "I didn't really understand, but I think she was asking about the weather."

"The weather, Tracy?"

"She said something about a shower."

"The shower!" Charlotte shouted, suddenly sober. She rushed to the phone.

Aha! Not *a* shower, *the* shower. The bridal shower. As the matron of honor, I considered that my responsibility, but Charlotte insisted on relieving me of the burden under the pretext that I lived too far away. Doubtless, she was remembering my somewhat riotous shower when she made that gesture, but that wasn't fair. I was the guest of honor, not the one who planned it.

I didn't catch up with her until she was just hanging

up with this Julie-person.

"Now I'll have to call the rest of the guests and put them off, too," Charlotte said. "What will they think?"

"I'll call them."

"Thank you, Tracy, but it's better that I do it. I'll know what to say."

I struggled to remember my promise of generosity.

"But you could do something for me, dear. Would you make me some coffee?"

I remembered it now and was kind enough not to meet her eyes. But all that generosity strained at my limit. I had to get something for it. While searching the kitchen for coffee filters, I came upon a ring of extra keys. One little brass beauty was labeled "attic." Suddenly, I knew where I might find the answers I needed.

"Charlotte," I said, when I returned with the coffee, "I loaned a book to Philly, and I really need to get it back."

Concentrating on her Rolodex, she asked, "Is that why you wanted to find him?"

I let her think so. "Would you mind if I looked for it?" I held my breath.

"Go ahead, Tracy." She dialed a number and squared her shoulders for the ordeal. "Look anywhere you want."

Where is it written a good deed has to be its own reward?

24

Amazing. People don't usually give me blank checks as Charlotte did; at least, not when they know me. It was just as well she didn't realize what I was up to. Though the meaning had become twisted over time, I still believed the old adage about ignorance being bliss. When other people were ignorant about my motives, my life *was* blissful.

While it wasn't my ultimate destination, I made a pit stop in Philly's room. Charlotte's cleaning crusade hadn't extended beyond this door. What a mess. Racing forms covered the unmade bed. Fragments of a broken pipe and empty matchbooks were scattered everywhere, along with most of the clothes Philly brought with him. Socks, under-wear — even his ratty suits. Though those were generally crushed into tight rolls so they retained their wrinkles, I suppose. The only suit missing seemed to be his brown tweed. A fine coating of ash dusted everything.

And I expected to find a clue to Philly's whereabouts in this clutter?

A bedside phone began to ring. I figured Charlotte would answer it downstairs, but that irritating bell wouldn't quit. I noticed Charlotte had put an old commercial telephone in the guest room with lights showing the two lines coming into the house. The light for one line remained constant, which probably meant she was on it downstairs. The other continued to flash.

Probably someone returning Charlotte's call. I'd be a sport and take a message, assuming she didn't object to my talking to her friends. Charlotte sure brought out the rebel in me. I blamed her for the adolescent and blasphemous greeting I gave the caller.

"Top of the world, God speaking." Clever little Tracy.

"Gotcha!" my mother said.

∞

The good news was that she no longer wanted me to come to Moscow. The bad news? She really let me have it.

"Tracy Lorraine Grainger!" Mother had come to adore Drew, but she never approved of my taking his name. "How dare you avoid my calls. You'd better watch yourself, miss, you're not too big to hit."

How long were her arms? She went on, really working herself up to a feverish pitch. Anyone else might have feared she'd have a stroke. Fortunately, I knew ugly scenes rejuvenated my mother; it was the secret to her long life.

"Cut me some slack, will you, Mother? I'm doing battle with life-and-death matters here." I knew telling her was a mistake as soon as I said it.

"Really?" Mother cooed. "Wedding off? Is Charlotte devastated? Tell me everything."

How much worse could it get? I told her.

She didn't sound the least contrite about her nasty remarks when I filled her in, but she decided to help. "So, darling, you need to find this man, Philly. He sounds delightfully colorful. Quite attractive, too, I imagine, for a man his age."

That meant she correctly figured that he was a shade younger than she was. "Mother, there's nothing you can do." I punched a pillow in frustration.

"Nonsense. Just give me a moment to roll this old goat off me. Alec," she shouted, "quit trying to cop a feel and go sleep on your own side of the bed."

Now *that* image would be burned into my brain forever.

"All right, darling, describe that room and don't leave anything out. Your father used to smoke a pipe, remember. I'll tell you how to find your pipe smoker."

∞

When I'd humored Mother long enough, I ended that conversation and went to the attic. No mess there. The only way Charlotte could have made my search easier would have been to hang neon arrows. Finding the family albums in boxes neatly labeled was nearly as good, however. There was even a comfortable old chair nearby. I flipped off the dust cover and settled down for a journey through time.

I couldn't resist catching a few glimpses of Drew in his various awkward stages. Any normal mother-in-law would have embarrassed her son with those pictures long ago. I paused over one snapshot of Drew's high school baseball team when they'd won the city-wide championship, and I picked my love's young face from the crowd. On the next page, captured under a plastic sheet, was an article the newspaper ran after Drew pitched his third shut-out of the championship season.

Drew still kept the old arm in shape, pitching for a law firm softball league when work didn't get in the way. He liked to say he could have tried out for the pros. We both knew his parents would have found that career choice nearly as alarming as Philly's. Besides, it worked out better this way. If he'd gone into baseball, he wouldn't have been visiting his law school roommate in L.A. the day I crashed into their car.

I gave the yellowing newspaper photo a gentle touch, then I exercised that infernal discipline I keep in check and found the album covering the school year my in-laws spent in Europe.

I have always found it heartrending to see a photograph of someone when they were much younger. The aging process should have shocked me less, as I'd been bombarded since birth by pictures of my parents at every age, but that only seemed to inure me to their changes.

Charlotte and Taylor looked so young in those photos, I felt ancient compared to them, even though they were around my present age. Taylor's hair hadn't begun to grey, and Charlotte looked slimmer than I'd ever seen her. There was one especially good shot of her in front of the Eiffel Tower wearing one of the fitted dresses fashionable then and looking like she was having more fun than I believed possible.

Interesting as they were, I hadn't wormed my way into that attic just to marvel at old photos. I was playing a hunch.

In that setting, I thought certain paths might have crossed. Another couple of pages proved me right. Captured forever were Zoya and Philly — young, together, and clearly in love.

I knew it! Sometimes you can feel when people once shared a relationship, especially when it didn't end well. As to the year — that was guesswork. Or maybe a sense that whatever they left unresolved had come back to haunt us.

Considering how I made the discovery, I wasn't in a position to criticize anyone else's honesty. But Zoya's lies infuriated me. I took petty pleasure that she seemed plumper than Charlotte in those pictures. Unlike Philly, who looked quite dashing, considering the aging teddy bear he'd become. Zoya shouldn't have let that one get away.

Confirming my hunches didn't make me feel better. Pandora never opened such a box. Could I close it again, even if I wanted to? I slammed the album shut. Philly held the key to this. I *had* to find him.

I remembered the suggestion Mother made. If her idea did the trick, she'd never hear it from me.

25

I stopped three people for directions, and I still got lost. Wouldn't you know it would happen the one time I shed my trusty sneakers? The heels I wore were depicted in their manufacturer's commercials as comfortable enough for playing tennis. Tennis, yes — walking two blocks without pain, forget it.

I wasn't clear on what part of the city this was. The Bowery, I suspected. I'd read that this area had undergone some gentrification; if so, they missed a pocket. Of course, every big city harbors neighborhoods like this. Places petrified with grime that reek of cheap beer, both before and after it's processed through the body. Where every other storefront is a bar and the kind that sports a neon cocktail glass when, in truth, a boilermaker is the closest they come to making mixed drinks.

I spied my destination, The Last Call. Where is it written those sleazy places have to sport cutesy names? I slowed my pace for a quick look through the front window before checking out the rear, though not slow enough to call attention to myself. Well, any more attention than the only woman in the neighborhood not living out of a shopping cart. I took a left at the corner and continued around the block, hopscotching over vagrants till I reached the alley behind the bar.

What was it with me and these alleys lately? This one made the shortcut behind The Gypsy Princess look like a corridor in Buckingham Palace. Nobody bothered with Dumpsters here, but that didn't mean they'd given up on garbage.

On my way back to The Last Call, I slipped into the character I planned to play for my entrance. I had borrowed a cocoa knit twinset and matching skirt from Charlotte's closet; nothing I owned captured the WASP princess look quite so well. For once, I was actually clean enough to play that part. Naturally, that happenstance occurred in a place from which I was unlikely to emerge in the same shape. I even exchanged my canvas backpack for my black purse. Not only didn't the backpack work with Charlotte's knit outfit, after taking it into the Dumpster, it reeked.

Pulling my collar into the upright position so fashionable with the country club set, I affected a manner that suggested my natural superiority allowed me to rise above this wretched place. Okay, so I was doing Charlotte — my generosity didn't extend this far.

When I described the contents of Philly's room for Mother, she zeroed in on the discarded matchbooks, reminding me how often pipe tobacco goes out. While some pipe smokers favor lighters, many prefer an old-fashioned match. They always grab promotional matchbooks, Mother insisted, especially since matches were becoming rare in this smokeless society. Five of the six matchbook covers in

Philly's room featured The Last Call, while one advertised a sundry shop in the Port Authority Terminal. If nothing else, that led me to wonder how long Philly had really been in New York.

I strolled through the door like I owned the place, wandering past the lost souls filling its chairs as if I hadn't noticed they were fellow human beings. I wiped the surface of a bar stool with a tissue before sitting. The massive man behind the bar, who looked like his face might have been rearranged in a boxing ring, glared down his crooked nose at me.

"You want a drink, lady?"

I gave him Charlotte's best *surely-you-jest* expression. "I'm looking for someone. Philly Chase."

"Philly Chase . . . " He did a bad imitation of someone searching his memory.

I produced a twenty-dollar bill and held it in the clumsy manner of a bribing novice who half fears she will offend the recipient, half that their fingers will touch and she'll need disinfecting. The scene played so badly, it belonged on network television. In the expected amount of time, his memory jarred.

"Yeah, I know him," the giant said.

"Can you tell me if he's been here lately?" I kept my voice strictly mid-Atlantic, losing the California twang.

"No, Philly ain't been around much."

"If you see him, would you kindly ask him to call his family?" I waved the twenty.

"Sure, why not?"

I nodded my thanks and dropped the bill on the bar, hopefully sending the message that I was a person who didn't soil her hands with anything as dirty as money. Right. After strolling out, I crept back and peered through the window. The bartender was placing a call.

I raced around the corner to the bar's back-door. Suddenly, it occurred to me that, without a Dumpster, I didn't have a place to hide. Attached to the side of the building was a corroded fire escape ladder. I reached for it and gave it a pull. That ladder was supposed to glide nearly to the ground, but this one was rusted in place over my head. Though I hadn't done a chin-up since junior high, I grabbed the lowest rung and dragged myself up until I reached the level where I could climb. Exertion made my arms tremble so much I feared I would fall. I clung to the ladder with a death grip.

Somewhere within the building, I heard stairs moan under someone's weight, but the steps were springy until the last flight. Finally, the door below me inched open. I kept my hope at bay until a worn loafer with a torn tassel appeared through the opening.

Philly leaned out and checked the alley in both directions. Thankfully, he didn't look up. Then he crept away along the side of the buildings. I let him get close to the street before quietly lowering myself to the ground. Just as he turned the corner, I slipped behind him and tapped him on the shoulder. He must have jumped three feet into the air.

"Tracy! I thought Charlotte — I mean — how did you find me?" he squawked.

I smiled as if modesty prevented me from sharing that tale. No way was I going to acknowledge my helper's role. I slipped my arm through his, so he wouldn't think about escaping, and steered him back to The Last Call.

"Philly, isn't it time we shared some secrets?"

∞

"Sure I cleared out," Philly said. "Can you blame me? I knew they'd figured out I lied about selling my share of The Princess to this Al Dupont."

With cold beers in hand, we had claimed a large wooden booth in the back room of The Last Call.

"Not Du*pont*, Du*mont*. You said Dumont," I reminded him.

"See, I can't keep my story straight. How long did it take them?"

I must have answered with my face.

"That long, huh?" Philly asked.

"Be fair, Philly. They're used to taking people at face value."

He nodded with compassion. "Poor slobs."

Philly put his head back against the booth and sighed deeply. He absently reached into the baggy pocket of his tweed jacket where he usually kept his pipe paraphernalia, but he grimaced as he pulled out a pack of cigarettes and a yellow Bic.

"Cigarettes?" I asked.

"Yeah. I left my pipe somewhere."

I could have told him where, but I didn't.

He lit a cigarette, drew the smoke in quickly and deeply, then sent it back out in one forceful burst. The smoke singed my nostrils — that was a first. I still longed for its familiar comfort. He placed the pack on the table between us. It was slightly crushed and only about half full, so the lighter sunk into a little valley within it.

In my own ragged state, I experienced a strange desire. The need existed on a purely visceral level, yet it consumed me. I felt an urge to *hold* the pack and the lighter. It was my hand, not my mind, that imagined how it would feel to wrap my fingers around that soft, crushed pack so the curve of the lighter pressed into my palm. I only wanted to pick them up, just that, but I wanted it badly. I *lusted* for it.

Well, maybe not *just* that. Naturally, I'd have one — but only one. Then I'd be off them forever. Come on, I was wasted. Didn't I deserve something? How could just one cigarette hurt?

But I knew. I squeezed the beer bottle so tightly I thought the glass would shatter. I struggled to remember why I was there and waited for the feeling to pass.

"You didn't really sell your share, did you, Philly?" My voice sounded tight.

"Yes, I did, I really did."

"So why the big secret about the buyer?" I asked.

"That's none of your business," Philly snapped with uncharacteristic sharpness. "I'm not going to tell you who bought it, Tracy, so don't even ask."

I found I could gradually ease my grip on the bottle.

"And if that's a condition of our talking, kid, then this conversation is over."

"Philly, you're playing a dangerous game with Marisa's life"

"Do you think I'd let anything happen to her? I can get the share back, and if I have to, I will. But I've been waiting."

"For what?" I asked.

He took his time deciding what to feed me instead of the truth.

"For you," he announced at last.

"Me?"

"I read your books. With all you know about investigating, I figured you wouldn't sit on your hands like the rest of them."

Philly paused to assess whether the hook was securely in the gum. I kept him guessing.

"Charlotte hates your books, you know. Well, really that you *write* them. She thinks everyone should have stopped writing after Shakespeare. That way we could revere the classics without knowing any artists." He wrinkled his nose in dead-on imitation of Charlotte at her most fastidious. "My sister will never understand what you're capable of, but Taylor says you're as tough as a bulldog."

How nice that my in-laws held me in such high regard.

"I figured you'd be looking for Marisa," Philly concluded. "Aren't you?"

I nodded.

"Find her — yet?" He gave me a hopeful, cockeyed smile.

"Do you see her? Cut the bull, Philly. You're exaggerating my abilities more than I do. The author makes it work in a book. In life, it's harder. We don't have much to go on, and we're almost out of time."

"What are you saying, kid?"

"That I need help, of course." Was he dense?

"Drew?" Philly asked.

"He isn't quite ready to volunteer." No one had spotted icebergs in hell.

His jaw dropped. "Tracy, are you asking me?"

My guess would be people didn't often count on Philly. I wasn't sure if I should, but at least I'd know where to find him.

"Yes, Philly, I am."

"As long as you know . . . " His voice trailed off but made clear his condition that I respect his one area of privacy. I didn't imagine Philly often felt that strongly about anything.

"I understand," I assured him.

"Then we're partners." Philly extended his hand over the middle of the table.

"Partners," I agreed with a firm shake.

I didn't feel as tense anymore. Was that because I felt secure in this relationship? Or that after all this smoke-free time, I had finally become a nonsmoker.

Bob, the bartender, a nice guy beneath that scary face, checked if we wanted another round. Philly told him we'd settle up. He patted his pockets.

"Uh . . . Tracy . . . ?"

I paid for our drinks and passed fifty dollars to Philly for his expenses.

He waited.

I sighed and fished out another fifty.

"Thanks, Tracy."

Terrific. He wasn't too proud to take my money as long as there was enough of it.

"I'll pay you back, kid."

The words sounded automatic. I wondered how many

times he'd made that promise, but knew I couldn't count that high.

"I know you don't *think* you will, Philly, but I *know* so."

26

Day's end — or so I wished.

I entered The Last Call and headed back to "our" booth, swinging my purse with carefree abandon. Or maybe because I couldn't steady my hand. My legs shook so badly, I hoped they didn't collapse under me.

"Beer, Tracy?" Bob called.

Make it bourbon and keep 'em coming. "I'd rather have coffee, Bob."

"I'll make a fresh pot."

I collapsed into the booth. Resting my head against the high wooden backing, I closed my eyes and tried to block it out. Didn't work. My mind's eye kept projecting gory images in vivid colors, mostly red. I placed my favorite black purse on the table before me for a post mortem. Drew gave me that purse for my last birthday. My favorite kind, too, a simple shoulder bag with no one's name, logo or phone number plastered anywhere on it. Only now it had a small, round hole on both sides.

Since I last saw Philly, I'd spent hours hunched over the computer and microfilm reader in the Fifth Avenue Library.

We split the work. My task was to explore the enigmatic Mr. Hunt's background, while Philly tackled his perplexing interest in restaurants.

Time got away from me. When I realized I might be late meeting Philly, I raced from the library. If I'd grabbed the cab that let a passenger out at the foot of the steps, my purse and I would have arrived in one piece. But I hadn't eaten in hours. The smell carried on the wind from the peanut roaster across the street beckoned.

Poised on the curb, waiting for a break in traffic — I heard an explosive blast. Before it registered that the sound wasn't a backfiring car, a bullet had passed through my purse. I was lucky. The shot hit low and wide, and it went straight through the leather without meeting anything that would alter its path. But the force of it knocked me into the road — right in the path of a speeding car. What were the odds of beating a bullet only to see my head crushed like a grape?

I would be eternally indebted to that man for maintaining his brakes. Nearly enough to forgive him for chewing me out for being stupid enough to get shot in front of his car.

No question about it, personal jeopardy was one of those things that read better than it lived. I made Tessa handle it with such aplomb, I never realized it would rattle me. Were we all dealt a finite number of close calls? Like a cat with its nine lives? Did what happened today constitute one close call or two?

When you glimpse the hereafter, you can't help thinking about how those you'd leave behind would live without you. If I were to die, Drew would never be the same. That's not to say he'd be grief-stricken — although he'd better be. I meant all my hard work would be lost. He'd revert to type. He'd start keeping endless lists again, and fun wouldn't be on any of them. Hard as it was, I had to stay alive, if only for his sake.

The sacrifice I planned to make for him must have preoccupied me. I didn't notice Philly had entered the bar until he popped into the booth. My body stiffened defensively. What was I thinking? Philly might pick my pocket, but did I really believe this sweet man would callously plot my death? But who else knew where to find me?

He slapped his hands on the table. "Kid, I hit the mother lode. I learned why our boy needs restaurants."

"You also found your pipe, I see." Even with his hand cupped around it, I would recognize that pipe anywhere.

"Yeah, I remembered where I left it."

"Where, Philly?"

"Another bar."

Sure.

"Beer, Philly?" Bob called.

"No time, Bob. I just stopped by for Tracy." To me he said, "You gotta see this for yourself."

"Tracy hasn't had her coffee," Bob argued.

"Don't worry, where she's going, there'll be plenty."

☙

It surprised me to see Nuri's cab waiting for us outside the bar. I had given Philly his dispatcher's number in case he found himself in a transportation jam. I must have been demented. Philly promptly booked Nuri for the entire day.

"The subway's too crowded. I'm running a tab with Nuri's boss," he said. "It doesn't pay to be cheap."

Sure, when it's not your money.

"Did you turn anything up?" he asked, as Nuri navigated through the city.

I hesitated, but decided not to tell Philly about the shooting. If he was the shooter, I didn't need to. If not, why put his limited courage to the test? Something told me that when the going got tough and the tough got going, Philly Chase would be long gone.

Instead I said, "Nothing conclusive, but I picked up some interesting bits about Hunt."

I also explored Zoya's background. As the offspring of major media manipulators, I had to admire her ability to generate coverage. Too bad she couldn't keep it consistent. At various times, she claimed to be everything from a Romanoff Grand Duchess to a ruling member of a nomadic Romanian minority group to just about everything in between, though most tended to include some suggestion of royalty. I wasn't sure whether the stories were a public relations miscalculation or the delusions of a troubled woman.

"So what do you think?" Philly asked.

It took me a second to realize he was asking about Hunt, not Zoya. It wasn't easy keeping their various relationships straight.

"It was just as I remembered. Hunt appeared from nowhere, threw up a couple of New York buildings, and slapped his name on both in big, splashy letters. Before long, he was the business magazines' favorite cover boy. Interestingly, he had no partners in those early projects. Today he sells countless shares, and they tend to change hands even during construction. You'd think it would have been the reverse, that he would have needed more money at the start. Where did he get the bucks he needed?"

Philly's eyes twinkled, but he said nothing.

"I also read up on his latest project. A luxurious Midtown complex of offices, apartments, and shops, all packaged with the tasteful tag, *Village de Hunt*. It's hard to understand, but this guy never has any trouble buying up almost everything in sight. There's still one holdout left on this project." I remembered what Weaver said about the fate of one competitor in the past, the businessman whom Weaver hinted Hunt had killed. I hoped history didn't repeat itself. "But Hunt only bought the rest of the property within the last six months, if you can believe it."

"Cutting it a little fine," Philly agreed.

"Actually, a large part of the area came on the market a couple of years ago. A company called Discovery Development acquired it at that time, then turned it over to Hunt several months ago for virtually no profit."

We exchanged suspicious glances, but I thought I saw wariness creep into Philly's. I'd tried to trace Discovery Development's principals, but I ran out of time at the library. Exactly how much money was Philly putting aside for his retirement?

"The other properties on the *Village de Hunt* site were all held by different individual owners. Most caved in quickly. Now there's only one left, the grandson of the man who originally built the building. The financial reporters don't hold much hope for him. The majority of his tenants have left, and while a few have suggested Hunt pressured them, they weren't willing to be quoted on it."

Hunt didn't seem to have any limits. I hoped he stopped short of kidnapping. Marisa wouldn't have been any safer with him than Briachi. I turned to the window to hide my fears from Philly. For the first time since we left the bar, I noticed my surroundings.

"Philly, we aren't far from the *Village* site. Would you mind if we took a look?"

Philly instructed Nuri to take a detour. Nothing had been razed on the site, but signs marked the perimeter. How arrogant. How could Hunt be sure the last guy would sell? It was easy to pick out the holdout building. It was the only one with some lights. The business day was not over; however, most of its windows were dark.

"How can Hunt keep pulling this off?" I asked, outraged. "Taylor told me New Yorkers consider this land Holy Ground. No one touches an inch of it without a fight."

I should not have said that holdout building was the only one with lights, it was the only one with *electric* lights. I saw the shadowy, flickering light of a candle on the second floor of a building a couple of doors away. For a moment I wished the squatters holing up there would burn it down and tie up Hunt's construction, but that would just put more people in jeopardy and Hunt's crusades invariably claimed enough.

"Tracy, this is Lord Hunt we're talking about."

"And the rest of New York's developers are boy scouts? Come on, Philly. Tenant protection is strong in New York.

Projects take years to get through the planning office."
Unlike Southern California, where we take pride in tearing
down mansions just to slap bigger ones on the same lots.
"According to my research, Hunt has never had a construction strike, either. What are the odds?"

Philly tossed his hand in a throwaway gesture. "Then
he has curious friends. The mob runs the building trades
here."

Was he sure about that? Was that the connection between Hunt and Tony's father?

Somewhere nearby, another construction site called it
a day. Instead of the usual single-blast quitting bell, some
patriotic foreman was attempting to play "This Land Is
Your Land" with the bell. The guys and I cracked up. I
didn't know about Philly and Nuri, but it was my first laugh
of the day.

"Tracy, I thought you of all people would know rules
are made to be broken." Philly's graying stubble twitched
with disappointment.

I knew many rules could be bent. I'd been stretching
them all my life. I also knew the difference between right
and wrong, more or less. And that some rules were as un-
bendable as granite.

"What do you do, Philly, when a rule refuses to break?"

Philly gave his bushy eyebrows a comical wiggle. "Easy,
kid. You give it another tap."

A tap? I pulled my purse close to my side. Call me
obsessive, but I was still hung up on that shooting. Was
that how Philly would describe what happened to me?

∞

We had arrived at our mysterious destination.

"A coffee shop?" I asked.

"Not just a coffee shop — it's one of Hunt's."

That piqued my curiosity, but at first glance I didn't find its ownership lent the place any visible distinction.

"Wait for us, Nuri," Philly said.

"Gotcha, Philly," Nuri called.

Now the little cherub had corrupted Nuri. I wanted to do that.

Philly took my arm and led me to the door. "Come on, Tracy. And keep your eyes peeled."

"For what?"

"Kid, you'll know it when you see it."

Drew would have refused to budge without a better reason, but I had a healthier regard for the game. I gave Philly plenty of rope, believing in good time he'd wrap up an explanation. Besides, there was food in there.

I ordered coffee and a tuna sandwich, assuming that would be fast. Philly just asked for a piece of cherry pie.

"Don't eat too much, Tracy. We won't be staying long."

Now he was getting into dangerous territory — between me and my dinner. "How will that be decided?"

"Depends on how quick you are."

Philly enjoyed having one up on me. He was so cute when he gloated, like an uppity teddy bear. When a weary waitress in a soiled gold-taffeta uniform tossed my sandwich before me, I really tore into it, though I didn't give the process full attention. I scrutinized everything, as my partner advised, but I didn't get it.

It looked like an ordinary coffee shop. Chrome counter with red leatherette stools, booths along the other side, worn grey-vinyl flooring. Not too fancy, not too seedy. Variations on decor aside, it was the kind of place you'd find in any town in the country. The only eventful thing that happened, if you could call it that, was that a man left his suitcase behind. He placed it on the floor next to the register while he paid, but he walked out without it. The cashier noticed it, but was too late to catch the man and instructed a busboy to put it in the office.

"You seen enough?" Excitement made Philly fidgety.

I laughed. "I haven't seen anything."

He couldn't hide his superior smile. "Come on. Let's go somewhere else for your dessert."

I hadn't finished even half of my sandwich. But I paid for it and Philly's uneaten pie, and we took our cab to another of Hunt's coffee shops. This one was equally non-descript, though it had an interesting neighbor. There was a fabulous toy shop next door that, while small, had wonderful displays. One window was filled with about a million tiny mechanical mice running amok. They appeared to be battery powered and directed through electronic chips, so they didn't run down like the old-fashioned, key-wound kind. I paused transfixed before it.

"Ready, Tracy?"

I pressed my face to the toy shop window, sighing wistfully. "This place looks like it would be more fun."

"Young lady," Philly said with mock severity, "we are not here to have fun."

"Too bad, huh?"

"Yeah," Philly agreed.

But duty called, for a reason that was not yet clear to me. We settled at a table, and I continued to play Philly's pointless little game. Or was it? Oddly enough, someone left a large cardboard box in this place. Again, it was placed in "the office."

"Let's move on," Philly suggested, his grin growing broader. "It's hell keeping you filled."

Some joke. Two restaurants, and I'd scarcely taken a bite. We entered the third place just as someone else was leaving.

"Is that your suitcase?" I pointed at the object left where he had been standing only a moment before.

"Huh?" the man grunted.

"There's a suitcase next to the cash register. Did you leave it there?" I asked, every inch the Good Samaritan.

If looks could kill, his would have completed the work begun by the bullet that came my way earlier. He shared a look with the young cashier with three steel studs in her nose.

She was quicker than he was. "Mister, you did leave your suitcase. I'll get it for you." She tried to pick it up, but it was too heavy. She finally succeeded in dragging it to the man. "Thanks for noticing, lady," she said to me warmly.

"Yeah, thanks," he echoed, less so.

"Seen enough, kid?" Philly asked.

"Yup. Let's go some place where we can eat without adding another penny to Hunt's coffers."

We let Nuri go home to his family and walked to another restaurant.

"Any idea what's in those suitcases and such?" Philly asked.

"At a guess — money. He's laundering money." The conclusion flabbergasted me. "The man actually built a development empire as a smokescreen for laundering money. He uses the restaurants to bring the cash in and the developments to process it."

And Zoya suggested he was too high profile to traffic in drugs. I wrestled with the gaps. They couldn't make all the exchanges with suitcases; people would notice. It was probably a coincidence that we'd seen so many of the same vehicles at one time. Still, I felt a similar arrogance in this setup as I had in the man himself. This was one area where the little thug's creativity would excel.

"Explains a lot, huh?" Philly asked.

More than he knew. I no longer wondered where Hunt found the money to start. Who had a greater need to launder cash than Organized Crime? Finally, the connection between Hunt and Briachi made sense.

With all they had at stake in this operation, they couldn't let anyone get in their way. I'd poked that hornet's nest with a stick, and someone took a shot at me — do the math. If I had any sense, I'd run for cover.

27

I dragged myself back to the townhouse. Voices buzzed in the living room, but I wasn't up to seeing anyone. I stashed my purse in the hall closet, where Drew wouldn't find it. Then I slipped down to the suite. I flopped on the bed, exhausted, but too wired to sleep.

The phone rang. Since Mother rarely repeated her games, I wasn't avoiding calls anymore. But I figured someone upstairs would answer it. When they didn't, I crawled across the bedspread toward the bedside phone with a martyred sigh. Dumb move. You'd think I'd learn I had two parents. Now it was Dad's turn.

"Tracy, your mother's hitting on the director and making a damn fool of herself," he said over international static and raucous background noise. "You gotta come here and put a stop to it."

Please, tell me I'm adopted.

"The woman has no shame. She must go to him in the middle of the night," Dad shouted over a burst of laughter. "The other night she threw me to the opposite side of the bed. What was she doing when she pushed me away? You know your mother and I have always slept with our limbs entwined."

Another image I'd never forget! "How would I know that? Why do you two persist in putting me in the middle of your relationship?"

Dad assumed a tone appropriate for the mentally deficient. "Baby, you are in the middle. You're the child."

Not wanting to run the risk of being saddled with another helper, I didn't tell Dad that Mother had been working with me that night. But I think I convinced him she wasn't stepping out — and prayed to the gods that it was true.

I listened to the background sounds. What time was it there? It sounded like he was eating breakfast with the crew, as he typically did. I asked Dad if I could talk with the prop man in charge of the production company's weapons, attributing my interest to research. In a moment, someone named Dusty Cooper came on the line.

"Dusty, could you give me a short course on long-range rifles?" I asked. "Pricey ones — for someone who can afford the best."

He did.

∞

Dad had said his good-bye several minutes before, but I continued to hold the phone to my ear until the telephone company's mechanical voice came on, rather than sever that connection. It wasn't my father I was trying to hold onto, but my life before all this began. I had to admit it — I was running out of steam. There was something about this case I was missing, but I couldn't pull it together. I kept waiting for a flash of inspiration, the kind that hits like a bolt of lightning. Inspiration eluded me. Funny, huh? I'd spent my life worshiping at the feet of Spontaneity, only to find, when I really needed it, that it had run off with the collection plate.

New York was getting on my nerves, too. I hated that it was never quiet, that the car horns wailed all night, that the sidewalks were so dirty — that it bulged with too many damn people! I had to be nuts, but I missed my parents. I missed my home! A place where palm trees sway in warm breezes and the Pacific laps gently against the shore — where we shoot at each other from cars, not rooftops, as nature intended.

I breathed a tremulous sigh. Somehow I had to keep going. For Marisa's sake. If I didn't find her, no one else would.

I rose to join the others upstairs, only a violent force of nature blocked the doorway. Hurricane Drew.

"Where have you been?" Drew demanded. "My mother said you'd called to say you were having dinner with a friend. Other than your editor and your fans, what friends do you have in New York?"

With his eyes rimmed in red and his cheeks hollow, he didn't look any better than I felt.

"Drew, don't you have more to worry about than my social life?"

He sighed and the starch went out of him, too. He collapsed on the edge of the bed. "Don't remind me. The kidnapper called with the final arrangements, and Tony taped the conversation. He's on his way over with it."

"Oh." I felt like I had the wind knocked out of me. I

sank into the spot next to Drew.

Well, that was that. All the tension I'd been carrying formed a cold pang of disappointment in my gut. Even without hearing the tape, I knew what it would say. I'd run out of time. With a few more days, Philly and I could have done it, I knew we could. We were making progress. But without knowing where Marisa was being held, the rest meant nothing. I wrapped my arms around myself for comfort. Out of time and out of ideas.

I'd failed — and Marisa lost.

∽

No one else seemed to be around when we went upstairs, but the doorbell began to ring. Drew answered it while I went to the den to pour myself a glass of red wine from an open bottle. Drew and Tony swept in after me, apparently continuing a conversation begun at the door.

"You're right, Tony. We have to find Philly," Drew said. The statement burned with intensity.

Excuse me? I just stood there, the bottle in one hand and the cork in the other, too stunned to speak.

"Did I hear someone saying something about Philly?" Charlotte asked from the doorway. "If only we could find him. Tracy, weren't you saying something about him just recently?"

That was too much. By rights, they should all have had sand on their faces.

Taylor followed on her heels. "You won't find him, Charlotte, unless he wants to be found." He came to the bar and took the bottle from my hand and poured himself a drink.

Charlotte took Taylor's glass for herself, so he poured another glass of wine. The last drink in the bottle.

"I'm afraid you're right, Taylor," she said. "The only person who could find Philly would be someone just like him."

Shouldn't I resent that? I turned my attention to Tony, who popped a cassette into the tape deck. He avoided making eye contact with me, as people often do after embarrassing confidences. The circles around his eyes were so dark, they looked more like shiners, but his expression seemed less tormented. I wondered whether his secret trip to the old homestead had anything to do with it.

All conversation ceased when Tony started the tape.

"Listen good. I'll say this only once," the kidnapper said.

Now I understood Tony's confusion about the caller's gender and age. The voice sounded like one of those fake kid's voices in radio commercials with just the slightest grain from cigarettes or whiskey. Since the call was made from a public phone, street sounds further obliterated it.

Even without asking, I knew the call must have come through at rush hour. The traffic sounds were too insistent for any other time, even in New York, where those sounds never died.

The caller gave precise instructions for how the transaction was to be carried out. This wasn't your usual cliché-riddled kidnapping. No money in small bills was to be left in a suitcase out on the Old Pass Road. She ordered Tony and the third owner of The Gypsy Princess to present themselves at the office of a particular attorney the following morning. The paperwork, already signed by Marisa, would be ready. And so would Lord Hunt's check.

The attorney didn't know anything about the nature of this deal, the kidnapper went on to say. And he wasn't to be informed — or Marisa would be killed. No one else was to be told — or Marisa would be killed. Blah, blah, blah — or Marisa would be killed. On and on she went, repeating that same deadly refrain in her chain-smoking kindergarten voice.

From out of the background, I suddenly heard a sound that meant something to me. Above the blended din of engines and voices and car horns were the unmistakably fractured notes of "This Land Is Your Land" played on a steam whistle. I was *there*. Philly and I had been right in that neighborhood when the call was made.

The kidnapper prolonged the call a moment longer, since she was caught by a consuming, down-to-the-soles-of-her-feet cough. That sweet child was developing emphysema.

"You see, Tracy, that's what people sound like when they've been smoking too long. Aren't you glad I nagged you to quit?" Drew said stupidly, probably just to have something to say.

A smoker . . . emphysema.

In that neighborhood.

Stunned, I threw my hand over my mouth: hyperventilation. I must have sounded like Darth Vader. Without a thought, I bolted from the room and from the house. I had slowed long enough to grab my purse but not a jacket — and it was cold outside.

In my present state, I didn't notice. I ran all the way.

28

A barefoot Weaver opened his apartment door. It seemed funny to see him in faded jeans and an old T-shirt from a 10-K race.

Breathing like an obscene caller, I struggled to catch my breath. "You said I should stop by for a little chat."

"I meant — " He waved a hand as if to say, *Forget it*. "Come on in."

While the apartment was spacious, with its homespun fabrics and raw woods, it had a rustic feel. Weaver's fantasy Southern home with the New York skyline plastered across the windows.

He led me into a den filled with bookshelves that looked like he built them himself. The Weavers seemed to have found a workable balance between his average salary and her spectacular income. The Tessa Graham Mysteries were prominently displayed on those shelves, I want it known. He showed me to an unvarnished red oak chair.

For once, Weaver was remarkably direct. "You 'bout ready to plop that big ol' thing in my lap?"

"*I'm* ready. I just need a little help getting *it* into position." I caught myself gripping the wooden arms of the chair. I couldn't let him see how badly I needed his help.

I explained what I wanted: A whole bunch of cops who would go where I wanted, when I wanted — without asking any questions.

Weaver snorted in disbelief. "You don't ask much, do you, Tracy?"

"This will get you put back in Homicide."

"It'll get me busted to Traffic."

"Weaver, you look like a risk-taking kinda guy."

His eyebrows rose in disbelief above the top of his glasses. "We both know I look like an accountant. A cautious accountant, at that. Sure, I'll take risks. What cop doesn't? That doesn't mean I'm crazy or oblivious to the hierarchy and rules. Running the plate, that was one thing. But this is something else. What you're asking can't be done."

He was less of a risk-taker than he had once been, and we both knew it. The last time he did something his superiors didn't like, they just slapped his knuckles. If he did it again, they'd probably chop his fingers off. Could I really expect him to jeopardize the rest of his career on my word?

Weaver stared out the window. "Tracy, you know how it's supposed to work? When I get a tip or run across a crime that's outside of my jurisdiction, I'm expected to refer the matter to the borough or precinct responsible for it."

Then why hadn't he passed down the tip on Philly to some precinct detective? That little cherub wasn't in the same league with the big boys Weaver's squad investigated. He didn't, because he thought Philly might give him another crack at Hunt. Hunt was still stuck in Weaver's craw.

"Detective, I can almost promise that you'll nail Hunt with this one." We both wanted the same thing. Why couldn't he see that?

His sigh sounded wistful. "If you could meet me halfway. Give me something I can bring back to the department to justify looking into it."

"I can't do that without breaking a promise." Drew and his parents would never forgive me if I told him. But if keeping that promise cost Marisa's life, I'd never forgive them or myself.

Weaver shrugged helplessly. "Then it's not going to happen."

I nodded to show my reluctant acceptance and headed for the door. He came around the desk and placed his hand lightly on my purse.

"Tracy, a buddy of mine said he followed up on a sniper report on Fifth Avenue today. Only when he arrived, there was no sniper and no victim."

He was uncomfortably observant. Unless he was on your side — and he wasn't on mine.

"Any truth to that report?" he asked.

"Why ask me?"

I offered to show myself out. I closed the door to his den and walked down the hall to the door. Just as I reached it, Leila popped out of the kitchen.

"Tracy, I didn't know you were here. Did you have some business with Jay?"

Obviously not. It occurred to me to wonder why I thought I should have had business with him. This official avenue wasn't my style. I would never have pursued it if the Eatons hadn't hamstrung me.

I felt a big grin replacing my despair. "Leila, why don't you walk me to the elevator?"

∞

I quietly crept into the suite, my arms full of packages, which I hid in the white lacquer cabinets that served as end tables in the sitting room. My caution proved unnecessary. I found Drew in the other room, stretched across the wrinkled bedspread, staring at the ceiling.

"Where did you run off to?" he asked without much interest.

"I remembered I had a book overdue at the library."

He didn't react to my answer. He had given up. Though I'd been close to losing hope myself earlier tonight, the big jerk still infuriated me. I dropped my purse on the night stand and crawled onto the bed. When I cradled him in my arms, Drew clung to me like a lifeboat in high seas. He didn't want love, just nurturing. Or so I thought. He started kissing me, desperately. That spark set off an inferno in me that consumed us both. Tearing at each others' clothes, we made love with an urgent, demanding hunger. Feeling every sensation as vividly as the first time. A celebration of life in the face of death.

∞

Good for what ails you. I curled up next to my sweetie, wearing a smile as big as Montana.

My sweetie didn't seem quite as thoroughly bathed in the afterglow. "My sister is being held against her will somewhere, maybe dying, while I — " He couldn't say it, but he gestured at me as if I were proof of his guilt.

"Give yourself a break, Drew. Everyone needs a little comfort." Especially me. I was knocking myself out for that family with neither recognition nor thanks.

Hastily, Drew crawled from bed and began to dress. "We must find Philly."

"Ah, we have returned to this evening's chorus, I see." I sat up and picked up my own clothes. No rest for the wicked in that house.

"As you suggested days ago," Drew added in the sing-song manner of a man paying extortion.

If I weren't such a good person, I could give lessons to Hunt. I waited. Drew still hadn't crawled enough.

He threw his mocha camp shirt to the floor in fit of anger. "You just can't let people save face, can you, Tracy?"

"*I told you so*, that's my motto," I said cheerfully.

"I thought it was, *Always keep score.*"

"What's the difference?" I asked.

We laughed as we hadn't since we arrived.

I took his hand. "Stop worrying, Drew. I have your uncle."

Mr. Hyde's transformation was swift and dramatic. "Did you go looking for him? Maybe when you *weren't* signing books?"

Nothing gets past him. "What's your point, Drew?"

"You gave me your word that you wouldn't look for Philly. Some people take that seriously." He yanked his shirt from the floor and marched into the sitting room.

I followed along reluctantly. "Some people take the *h* in *vehicle* seriously. Does that mean we all have to?"

Steam rose from Drew's ears. "I bet you've had him all along."

"I was the only one who cared that he was missing. Remember? And I just found him."

"How?" he asked, reluctantly giving in to curiosity.

"Wasn't easy, let me tell you." I described my search for Philly, embellishing the task, so that in difficulty it sounded like something that fell between climbing Mt. Everest and moving it.

Drew noticed he'd crushed his shirt in his hands. He went back to the bedroom to find something else to wear. "Has he admitted to lying about the buyer for his share in The Gypsy Princess? I bet he didn't sell it at all."

I followed along. "My guess, too, but he swears he did. He won't name the buyer, though." I described how tightly Philly guarded that secret.

Drew stuffed a crisp white shirt into his battered navy Dockers, in which the crease was now just a memory. How his standards were plummeting. "Tracy, you don't know Philly. Believe me, nothing is that important to him."

"Something is — this time. But stop worrying, Drew. He says he can get his share back if he needs to."

"He needs to!" Drew shouted. "Get him over here now. We'll make the arrangements tonight."

"There's . . . another alternative. Now I have to warn you, it's a little unconventional, but I think — "

"Oh, no. *No!*" he roared. "I'm not going to let you endanger Marisa's life with something that even *you* consider unconventional."

I'd had enough of all of them. "If anyone is endangering her life, it's you and your parents. You've put the family honor and your dirty little secrets above what's best for Marisa. Stop bellowing, Drew, and be honest. Would Marisa want you to sign away the most important part of her life? To Hunt? When there's another way?"

"If the kidnapper can be believed, she's already signed it away herself," he said, but without his usual obstinance; he knew I was right.

I took both of his hands in mine. "She had no choice, but she's counting on us to find one. Come on, Drew, she's the real Gypsy Princess. She'll never forgive us for selling her namesake."

For once, instead of reacting with instinctive resistance, he really looked into my eyes. All the way to where my thoughts were kept.

"Will your idea work?" he asked tentatively.

I hesitated, unsure of how to continue, now that I had him halfway there. "There's something you have to know before you commit to it, Drew."

"Nothing matters but Marisa."

"This does." I picked up my purse from the bedside table and stuck my pinkie through one of the bullet holes, from the inside, and waved it at him. It only took a moment before understanding crept over his face.

"If you didn't like it, Tracy, you could have exchanged it," he deadpanned.

"That would have been too easy."

He smiled shortly, then asked, "When would we do it?"

"Tomorrow morning." My voice sounded shaky.

Drew ran his fingers through his wavy hair. "That's when Tony's set to go to that lawyer's office. We won't get another chance."

"If it comes to that, Tony can still go — with someone who will present himself as the other owner." I was, of course, thinking of Nuri.

"A ringer? You want him to engage in fraud?" Drew asked.

In my next life, no way would I marry a lawyer.

Drew sighed and sank to the edge of the bed. He judged the spacing wrong and slipped to the floor. "Can he pull it off, this ringer of yours?" he said, looking up at me.

"I don't know." I knelt next to him. Now we'd come to the tough part. "Can he borrow your clothes?"

29

A truck pulled up outside the ghost town that would one day be known as *Village de Hunt*. One truck, then a motor home and a couple of minivans. People poured from all of them. Working men with lights, stout women with racks of clothing, one temperamental photographer in a cowboy hat and alligator boots, and no less than eight tall, beautiful women, one of whom was the world's most famous Southern Belle, Leila.

In dark clothing that blended into the shadows, Philly, Drew and I watched from the corner as the raucous fashion shoot set up outside the empty building where Philly and I had seen a flickering candle the day before.

Leila had really outdone herself. When I asked if she could provide a noisy distraction, I had no idea she would come up with anything this elaborate. How had she talked so many busy people into donating their time and effort — and at the last minute? Had she warned them, as I warned her, that it might be dangerous?

More importantly — had she kept it from her husband? Right up until the moment we left the house that cloudy, grey morning, I'd expected Weaver to knock on our door and call the whole thing off.

I wasn't sure my accomplices wouldn't have preferred that. There I was, a finely honed investigative machine — in the hands of two incompetent operators. Talk about tight. Philly's anxiety took the form of naked fear. "What ifs" flowed from his mouth like drool. What if we were wrong? What if we only scared the hell out of some innocent squatters? He wouldn't shut up! How could this man have had the guts to pull off some of his loony scams? Perhaps they'd never mattered this much. But still — where was that sprite now, that joyous man-child, that crook, when I needed him?

He'd performed beautifully last night. He showed up at the house waving a bottle of cheap champagne and cheerfully announcing that he'd tracked down the buyer of his share of the restaurant. This man, Dumont, he'd assured Charlotte and Taylor, would meet Tony at the lawyer's office tomorrow morning. And he hoped they understood about his rushing off without a word, but he remembered something his friend had said and couldn't waste a moment before acting on it.

Naturally, all was forgiven. Charlotte went so far as to say she always knew he was hunting for Dumont. "Didn't I say that?" she kept repeating, as if she'd been his lone supporter.

I should not have let the way they twisted the truth astound me. Even on the eve of the deadline, denial still ruled. Taylor was the only one to present a solution, and I questioned its practicality. He planned to forge a Letter of Intent from Dumont promising to sell and would post a bond for the full value of The Princess payable to Hunt — if the sale did not go through. I wondered why he didn't just go along with Tony and forge the name to the transfer papers, since what he proposed was equally fraudulent, but apparently that was the extent of his ethical flexibility. Since it was still enough to guarantee disbarment, I couldn't let him do it. But he would have risked even that to keep their deep, dark secret forever deep and dark.

Philly also made me nuts with his insistent demands to arm us more conventionally than I planned. To my amazement, Drew liked the idea.

"No guns!" I insisted.

Philly argued that I sometimes armed my characters, and I was forced to explain what people like us assiduously avoid — that real life could be a drag.

"Reality check, guys." I threw questions at both of them. "Drew, what's the penalty for carrying a concealed weapon? Philly, can your record stand that?"

"I've never been convicted," he said with obvious pride.

"Since you haven't saved for your retirement, this would be the ideal time to start. What about you, Drew? Doesn't the Bar Association frown on its members getting convicted of anything other than white collar crimes?"

We wanted Marisa's kidnapper to serve a huge amount of time behind bars, I reminded them, and that wouldn't happen if we did anything that jeopardized the case. My voice might have sounded waspish, but dammit, why did I have to be the adult? We had Drew for that.

My husband didn't disappoint me. He became even more rigid than Philly. His nerves emerged as righteous indignation directed at — who else?

"Look at you!" he said with shocked accusation, when he caught a hint of a smile on my face. "My sister's life hangs by a thread, and you're having a good time!"

I let him think so. After all, that was the shallow, devil-may-care Tracy he knew and occasionally loved. The truth was more complex than that. On one level, his charge was accurate. Despite the emotional ups and downs, despite the danger, I'd had a ball this last week. I was not about to act as if it had been a sacrifice. Why should doing the right thing have to feel bad?

But neither was I oblivious to the stakes involved. Not just Marisa's fate, either. There was Nuri and his family's status in this country to consider. As well as Drew's promise to his baby sister and how it would devastate him to feel he'd broken it. And those damned secrets. No matter what I thought of them, they weren't mine to leak. There were lives involved in more than the obvious ways. Self-images were on the line, the armor some people needed to face the world. And it was up to me to bring them through this intact. A heavy load rode on my nearly ethereal shoulders.

Eventually, my enthusiasm proved infectious. Or my co-conspirators saw the plan coming together. Leila's staged photo shoot was attracting the attention of the workers and others remaining in the buildings of the *Village* site, exactly as I had hoped. The few employees remaining in the holdout building gathered at their windows to watch the activity in the street. I threw a glance at the other building where I'd seen the candlelight and could just barely make out a human form standing close enough to the window to watch — but not close enough to be seen. Yes! That was what I thought we'd see. An innocent person would have gone right up to the window and enjoyed the spectacle at hand.

Excitement surged through me, and that ignited my troops. We were ready.

We made our way around the back. Drew held the door for us. While reading up on Hunt at the library, I noted the name of the man who had owned that candle-lit building until a few years before. When I called to ask about it, he admitted to going to see it only a few weeks before.

"Sentimental journey," he confessed. "It's a mess now. People have pulled up all the rugs, and they were good, thick ones, too. Now there are big spaces under the office doors."

Spaces? I remembered something.

The elevator wasn't working, he said, but he told me where to find the stairs. He even remembered some of the spots where the floors creaked.

The space he described between the bottom of the door and the cement floor sounded perfect for our purposes. But it would work against us, too. Every sound we made would carry back into that room. And in that empty building, footsteps, even in rubber-soled shoes, would echo like thunder.

By climbing the stairs single-file, stepping only on the sides of the risers where they would groan the least, we managed to minimize noise. We gathered at the end of the second-floor corridor and silently exchanged hand signals before putting it all in motion. The door to the front office was just ahead of us — but at the end of a what seemed like a very long corridor. We couldn't risk getting any closer.

I dropped to my knees and waved for the others to do the same. We slid along the sides of the hall, taking care not to catch ourselves on the strips of exposed carpet tacks. Just after we passed the halfway point, Philly signaled for me to stop. I wanted to inch closer, but this was his part of the operation. He and Bob had practiced distances last night on the floor at The Last Call. We slipped off our backpacks and began unloading our equipment.

I would have given anything for recessed doorways or twisted corridors, anyplace to hide. No such luck. Buildings of that vintage were designed with permanent suites and lacked some of the architectural flexibility of newer structures. But one old-fashioned touch proved useful. There were translucent glass panels in the office doors, like the ones in some old movies. When a shadow flickered behind that panel, I held my breath.

A sunnier day would have made a more distinctive silhouette. The shadowy one produced today wasn't enough to confirm that we'd come to the right place. Until the person beyond that door coughed. Not a little throat clearing, either. This was a consumptive bark like the one we heard on the kidnapper's tape. I silenced a relieved sigh.

Philly nodded when he was ready. Despite knowing what to expect, I nearly burst out laughing. Spread across the floor were hundreds of those little electronic mice he and I had seen in that toy shop window. Well, having ruled out guns, what else could we use?

Philly and I flattened ourselves to the floor and grabbed the remote controls. The night before, we had programmed twenty to respond to each control unit, and Philly and Bob had practiced until two in the morning, and now we sent those little suckers flying down the hall. Some crashed into the walls at our sides and lost their sense of direction, but most succeeded in slipping under the door.

"What the fuck?" a voice cried.

Heavy steps started for the door, slipped, but caught and continued.

The kidnapper threw the door open.

She *filled* the doorway.

She pointed a gun at us, her finger starting the squeeze on the trigger. But Drew was prepared. He'd already armed himself with a couple of the baseballs he carried in his fanny pack. Without an instant to spare, Drew pitched one right in. I thought his golden arm quivered in the windup, and I was right. The ball sailed past her ear.

The near miss was good enough to buy him some time. The kidnapper stared in astonishment, her finger easing on the trigger. Drew used the moment he'd gained to focus. His eyes narrowed in concentration, his lips tightened. The arm looked sure and steady when he drew back this time, and he fired it with all his might.

The fast ball connected. It knocked the gun from her hand with such force, the weapon fell to the floor and slipped down the hall, stopping between us and her.

Philly dove for it, but so did she. He managed to kick the gun away, but she landed on top of him — and the fight was on. She was bigger than Philly. Hell, she was bigger than Texas. But he held his own. Until she managed to land a jab under his chin. That stunned him. Only for a moment, but that was enough. She slipped her hands around his throat and squeezed with all the strength that giant body possessed.

Drew grabbed the gun, but the bodies were too close to risk a shot. Oh, God! I had to do something, but what?

Drew looked as helpless as I felt. *The bat!* I thought at last. I ran down the hall for the baseball bat we'd left in one of the backpacks, but I slipped on some of my own little mice and landed on my fanny. Drew finally took the gun and slammed it into the side of the kidnapper's head. That didn't faze her. I pulled myself up, whirled around, and threw a kick at her ribs. Neither did that. She just kept tightening the grip on Philly's throat.

Philly's face turned red. He gasped. He was only moments away from losing consciousness.

Drew grabbed the kidnapper around her throat. He squeezed just as hard. I snatched handfuls of red hair and yanked with all my might. It slowed her — but only a little. She would last longer than Philly — and we both knew it.

30

"Freeze!" a voice cried from the stairs.

Dozens of footsteps pounded up the stairway.

"Y'all get up real slow now, hear?" The cavalry had arrived in the form of Weaver and his troops.

"I hope you don't mind, Detective," I said breathlessly. "We got here early, so we started without you."

Two cops yanked the kidnapper off Philly. Philly gasped for air, but I watched him — until I saw the color coming back into his face. I flashed Weaver a grateful smile. Weaver, that naughty little eavesdropper, didn't know who he was dealing with. Then he saw the kidnapper's face. Now he took no chances — keeping his service automatic on her — even after she was cuffed.

There she was, the big redhead I'd once seen in a mug shot: Belle Cannon. The woman believed to have killed for the benefit of Lord Hunt. Weaver was right, we *had* met. Disguised as an old woman, she sat next to me on the plane flying there.

Mrs. Thomas Dodd from Bakersfield, California.

How could I forget that cough?

Stepping carefully over the mice, Drew and I dashed

into the office to look for Marisa. She was there, but talk about overkill. Not only was she blindfolded, gagged, and chained by her ankles to the floor, she was also deeply drugged. Weaver could not have known what to expect when he followed us into that office, but he didn't need any diagrams drawn for him, either. In an instant, he ordered one of his men to call for an ambulance and a locksmith.

One of the cops started dragging Belle off, but she pulled to a halt before me.

"A detective." Her lips twisted into an ugly sneer.

"Found you, didn't I?" I said smugly.

Then they took Belle downstairs. I looked out the window to see her exit. Squad cars crowded the block now. I noticed Weaver walked a little taller. Other cops tapped him on the arm and sprinkled words of congratulations. I didn't know whether he'd collected that force with the department's sanction or if everyone had sacrificed a day off. Either way, from their attitudes, I gathered Weaver's risk paid off.

They marched Belle into the street where a crowd had formed around the photo shoot, raising the noise level to record decibels. Then something sliced through the clatter.

A shot rang out. Then another.

I hit the dirt, or the floor in this case. Being fired on every day sharpens the reflexes.

But I wasn't the target — Belle Cannon was. The sniper nailed her, as well as one of the cops escorting her. I left Drew to watch over his sister and ran downstairs. When I reached Belle's side, she was bleeding profusely and her breathing sounded labored. She tried to speak, but no sound came out.

"Fan out!" Weaver ordered.

Police officers, wary of the sniper, spread in every direction. But no more shots were fired.

The ambulance arrived. The paramedics said the wounded officer would make it, and Marisa and Philly were in no danger. But Belle Cannon had died.

The net of officers draping the area cornered a man at a nearby building on a direct line with the spot where Belle was shot. It shocked them all, I could see, when they realized their suspect was the one and only Lord Hunt.

They found him on the side of a building. Not hovering in flight like Superman but ineptly climbing down the fire escape ladder, bad leg and all. He claimed he had been climbing *up*. Said he was supposed to meet someone on that rooftop to discuss a deal. A man in his position often met people in strange places, he insisted; he didn't say which position.

The evidence didn't bear out his claims. No one waited on the roof. There were, however, scratches on the gravel rooftop of the sort his bum leg made.

They also found a long-range rifle there, the kind a sniper might use. When a crime scene technician brought it down, I compared it to what Dusty Cooper, Dad's prop man, told me about long-range rifles. It had the same long, heavy barrel. It also featured a bolt action and carried a very small clip. The telescopic sight was mounted on the top of the rifle but on legs that elevated it above the iron sights, just as Dusty said.

It looked like an exact match for some of the rifles I saw in Hunt's office. He had done this before. If it was the rifle that fired on me outside the library, and the one Hunt once used to take out a competitor — I hoped he choked on it.

Dusty also said a rooftop sniper might rest the rifle on a small cradle that he propped on the parapet or at least on a sandbag that would elevate and steady it. They found a cradle up there, too. No sandbags for this guy. Nothing but the best for Lord Hunt.

Knowing they would discover the rifle was registered to him, Hunt didn't deny ownership. He insisted it had been stolen months ago and even reminded the officers he'd reported the theft. Anyone can report something stolen, Weaver said; that didn't mean it really had been.

The furor made when the District Attorney charged Hunt with murder and kidnapping was nothing short of atomic. They were already calling it the trial of the century. The latest one, at least. Weaver told me later that even though some of the prints found on the rifle were smudged, enough clear ones remained to nail to Hunt. The case, he assured me, was solid. Influence wouldn't help him this time.

I should have been thrilled. So — why wasn't I happy with the outcome?

31

The Eatons carried on as if nothing happened. Well, it was just so sordid, Charlotte explained, that it was really best to put it behind us and never mention it again. Since Drew, Philly and I low-keyed our role in the caper, we could hardly complain about her glossing over it.

Naturally, the wedding would go ahead on schedule. With so much remaining to be done, but so little time, the Eatons threw themselves into that task with nearly as much relish as they had plunged into denial. Well, not the whole family. They acknowledged that Tony and Marisa needed to rest. Corbett decided he wanted a short vacation in Paris before heading back. And naturally, Taylor had to return to his neglected law practice. That meant most of the work fell to Drew and his mother. Philly and I offered to help, but Charlotte declined with a polite shudder.

Taking his mother's petty orders did nothing to improve Drew's mood. He took it out on me.

"You told her you were a detective! Tracy, I hope you're sorry."

"What are you saying? That this person, who just happened to be disguised, took that as a challenge and went out and kidnapped your sister? Get real, Drew. Belle Cannon sat there to learn what she could from us."

"And didn't you provide her with plenty?" he asked.

Oops. Dangerous doo-doo ahead. That accusation was harder to deny. I had to face it: Someday when I ran out of my allotment of close calls, it will have been my big mouth that pushed me over the edge.

Philly went back to sleeping in the house, but he spent most of his days at The Last Call. He said that with Charlotte so energetic and directed, he was afraid if he stayed with her too long she'd transform him into a solid citizen before he knew what happened. Fat chance. He just liked talking with Bob.

I went with him a couple of times, but mostly I took long walks alone. The fondness I'd always felt for New York, which had wavered when I became discouraged, blossomed again. But I took no joy from being there. The truth was I felt a little flat, unsettled.

"You're just bummed because there wasn't any mystery. The most obvious suspect did it." Drew laughed. "Face it, Tracy, you hate anything ordinary."

Sure, that was it. But I knew how compulsive I could be. If I didn't tie up a few loose ends, I would never rid myself of this uncharacteristic deflation. Nothing important, really.

Once the police removed their seal, I went back to the room where Marisa had been kept. I looked at how the ankle chain was secured to the floor, and the locks on the door and the windows. The building had been sold to Discovery Development more than two years ago. When Discovery took over, tenants were asked to vacate as their leases expired. According to the newspaper account, the last tenant moved over a year ago. The windows in that office didn't look like they'd weathered more than a few months of sun and rain, and the sturdy brass deadbolt had only begun to tarnish.

I also returned to the rooftop where they found Hunt to study the scuff marks his footsteps made in the gravel. The police were right, you could trace Hunt's movements by the pattern. He walked from the fire escape to the parapet, where the shot was fired. Actually, he walked it twice. Up-and-back, up-and-back. Unless he had suddenly taken to dragging both feet. I wondered why he walked it twice.

As I said, just a few loose ends.

∞

Despite her ordeal, Marisa made a breathtaking bride. We waited at the house so we could be the first to see her in her gown. It seemed to capture the diverse qualities juxtaposed in this girl we loved. There was something of the exotic in the cut of the off-the-shoulder bodice and the vibrantly colored flowers that filled her bouquet, but the full satin skirt and long train were strictly traditional.

Drew beamed, and all the tension that continued to build while serving as his mother's pack mule seemed to go out of him. There in the house watching Marisa swirl down the stairs, rather than when we rescued her, it finally seemed to hit Drew he'd kept his promise to the baby who was once presented to him as his sister.

When we settled into the back of the limo taking us to the church, Drew put his arm around me and pulled me close. We shared a silent, congratulatory moment for what we accomplished.

"Marisa looked great, didn't she, Trace?" His voice held such satisfaction.

I assured him she did. I pressed my head against his shoulder and savored the warmth and sharing for a moment longer.

Then I leaned forward. "Excuse me, driver, we're going to make a little detour."

"What?" Drew asked.

I gave the driver directions.

"Tracy, what are you doing?" Drew spoke quietly, as if he was afraid of setting off an avalanche. Bad sign.

"I just want to stop a minute at the building."

"What building?" he demanded. Storm clouds began to gather in his eyes.

"You know, the one where we found Marisa."

"Now? You can't! We'll be late for the wedding."

He moved on to shouting. Avalanches be damned. Why did he let me exasperate him so? It couldn't be good for him.

"Drew, what are they going to do? Start without us? We're the secondary leads."

Over Drew's objection, we drove to the former *Village de Hunt* site.

"You can't go out there," Drew argued when the car stopped. "You're wearing your gown."

And . . . what? The bag ladies were going to object? If I didn't get him home soon, he was going to die this stiff.

I bolted from the car, but stopped short on the sidewalk. What was I thinking? I knew I couldn't go to the

Hall of Records before the wedding, but I thought I might catch some of the people working in that last unsold building. I'd hoped someone could answer the one question still gnawing at me. I forgot they wouldn't be working on the weekend.

Turning back to the car, I noticed a man standing before that building. I'd seen him from the start, but I thought he was a street person. His shoes were dusty, and a few days' worth of stubble covered his face, but the wrinkled camel-hair jacket he wore looked expensive. Besides, the way he stared at that building just broke my heart.

"Sir, do you own this building?" I asked on a hunch.

The man turned sorrowful green eyes toward me. "For the moment. My grandfather built it, you know, and he gave it to me. But I have an appointment with Lord Hunt's lawyers in less than an hour to turn it over to him." He looked ashamed as he said, "I can't hold out against him any longer."

The poor guy was so far out of it, he didn't seem surprised by personal questions from a total stranger in a formal gown.

"Where have you been for the last few days?" I asked.

"In a cabin I have in the Poconos. I just couldn't come back until the last minute."

I loved being the one to deliver the good news. "I don't think you'll need to keep that appointment. Buy a newspaper, then go home and get some rest."

He studied my face, first for understanding then to see if I really meant it. When he was convinced I did, he gave me a vague smile and a grateful nod.

"Wait," I called as he turned away. "That building two

doors down? A while back the former owner sold it to a company called Discovery Development. Do you happen to know who's behind Discovery Development?"

"You know, I do. It took a lot of time and money to trace the name, but I thought I might appeal to the owner not to sell to Hunt." He shrugged. "It didn't work."

"Would you tell me that name?" I held my breath.

He did.

32

They held the wedding for us. I told Drew they would.

When I walked down the aisle, I noticed the small, sad woman from Briachi's house huddled in a rear pew. Only today, at her son's wedding, she beamed with pride. Now I understood how Tony kept up with the gossip I thought he could have learned only at his parents' home. He met with his mother even after his name and accent change.

He also confirmed why he went back the day I crawled into the trunk of his father's car. He needed to confront the old man, to learn for sure whether his father was involved in the kidnapping of the woman he loved. Tony looked more at peace after he made that trip.

According to this morning's paper, Briachi's lawyers succeeded in cutting a deal, though he had Lord Hunt to thank for that. Briachi agreed to testify against Hunt in exchange for immunity and a new identity.

I felt sorry for Mrs. Briachi. If she stayed with her husband, as mobsters' wives were apt to do, she was going to lose her son. It seemed a poor trade. I shivered when I remembered the inhumanly callous expression on that man's face. Still, she hadn't left him in all those years. Poor Tony. No one apart from the few friends he'd made in his new persona sat on his side of the church. But he was getting a new family, such as it was.

The ceremony was enchanting, but being such a shallow party girl, I will always remember the reception best. Drew and I danced till we dropped, and I probably enjoyed myself more than at our own wedding, though no mothers came to blows at this one.

Corbett met a New York businesswoman in Paris and invited her to the wedding. He looked happier than I'd seen him in years. Hardly drank a drop, either; maybe that unhappy chapter in his life was ending.

I met Nuri's wife and found her to be a charming imp. I knew I couldn't have been the first positive influence in his life. Drew pressed his father to introduce Nuri to one of his developer clients, and it looked like he was going to be an architect again.

I also spent time with Jay and Leila Weaver. Charlotte didn't understand why we insisted on inviting all those last-minute guests. She still clung to the belief that the police came upon Marisa in the course of another investigation, and that Philly, Drew and I just happened to be in the neighborhood. For once, she was too happy to argue.

"You know something?" Weaver said. "Once you get past her fussy, Northeast-lady kinda ways, your momma-in-law's pretty nice." That seemed as good a way as any of describing Charlotte's character.

Weaver confirmed something I'd already figured out. The reason he believed I might be involved with Belle Cannon was that she'd handled the flight magazine I left in the holding room. Suspicious devil that he was, Weaver ran it for prints. He admitted he might be more open with people peripherally involved with his cases in the future and suggested I consider the same approach with the police — if our paths ever crossed again. Sure, that would happen.

He and I even sandwiched in a philosophical discussion. He raised a fascinating and classic point of law: Whether it was right to convict someone for a crime he didn't commit, when he got away with one he actually did.

"I think so," I said, "but I'm a writer, not a cop. I can shoot for a purer form of justice."

"Don't be so sure." Weaver smiled enigmatically. He might talk a little funny, but we shared the same wavelength.

Toward the end of the evening, I finally wrestled Philly away from all the women monopolizing him. I had stolen a little time from my lonely wanderings the last few days to drag Philly to the best Fifth Avenue salon. Once someone used shampoo and conditioner on his unruly hair, rather than a bar of soap, the beast was tamed. The rakish cut didn't hurt, either. I convinced Charlotte that he had to be outfitted in formal attire the same as the rest of the family, even if he wasn't in the wedding party. The dashing presence he made sure worked like a charm with the ladies.

I took him outside to the ballroom's balcony. It was cold out there, but we didn't notice. In companionable silence, we leaned against the balustrade and watched the Gypsy Princess twirling on the dance floor in her new husband's arms.

Philly took my hand in his. "We done good, kid. I'll never forget this day."

I studied Philly speculatively. "Her father must be very proud."

"Yeah, old Taylor's popping his buttons today," Philly said with in a gruff voice. He swallowed hard.

"I didn't mean Taylor, Philly — I meant you."

He dropped my hand. "Tracy, what are you saying? Are you suggesting I fathered a child by my own sister?"

"Charlotte isn't Marisa's mother." She wasn't pregnant before Marisa's birth. The pictures in the attic proved that. "She's your daughter, Philly. Yours and Zoya Vrescu's."

He quickly stoked the coals of his anger to strike out at me in flames, but the fire died almost instantly.

"I loved Zoya, Tracy. Enough to go straight for her and the baby. I thought she cared for us, too, but . . . " He finished the statement with a pitiful shrug. "We planned to be married, but Zoya put it off. She kept saying she had to be sure. When the baby came, she was sure all right — sure that she wasn't cut out for motherhood. She left Marisa with me and just took off. I would have done anything for my little girl, Tracy, but let's face it, without someone to keep me in line, what kind of life could I have given her?"

"You did the best thing you could for her, Philly. You made it possible for her to have a wonderful life." I spoke with all the sincerity I could muster so he would know how much I meant it. "You used Zoya for your Gypsy Princess story, didn't you?"

With a nasty chuckle, he said, "Caught that, did you? Zoya was always telling people her father was a Gypsy king."

"And about a thousand other things."

"But that was her favorite. I think she actually believes it. Who knows? That story might even be true." Philly turned away. He leaned his elbows on the railing while gazing at the lights of the Manhattan night sky.

"Yet — you sold her your share in the restaurant, didn't you, Philly?"

"Sold nothing — I *gave* it to her!" He sounded appalled by his own unprecedented generosity. "I went to see her months ago to tell her Marisa was engaged. It bothered me that she had no contact with her daughter, so I gave her my share in the restaurant. But she asked me to keep the transfer secret for a while. I was disappointed, you know? But I didn't think anything of it. Zoya's such a whiz in business, I figured she was just using it for extra leverage in some deal she was putting together." Philly sighed. "Now she doesn't want any part of The Princess. Her lawyer called me yesterday to say she was returning my share. Free of charge."

I placed a comforting hand on his back. "That share is back where it belongs."

Now that it was, maybe I ought to have a word with Corbett about putting it in some nonvoting trust. Seedy old grifters didn't make the most reliable of business partners, God love 'em.

"Doesn't matter." His bitter tone belied that. "Zoya doesn't want to see Marisa. That's all there is to it."

I took his hand and turned him around to face me. How was I going to tell him? "That isn't all there is to it, Philly."

"What do you mean, kid?"

"Hunt didn't engineer Marisa's kidnapping any more than he killed Belle Cannon."

"How can you say that? The cops caught him red-handed. He was coming down from that rooftop."

I shook my head. "He was going *up*."

"Tracy, they found his rifle there."

"It *had* been stolen, Philly."

"His footprints were on the rooftop," he said.

"*Someone's* were."

"Kid, this is nuts. Who else benefitted?"

"Doesn't that depend on the motive? Not everything is about money or gaining leverage in business. Philly, the Gypsy Queen had her revenge."

"You mean — Zoya?" He frowned, but I saw the spark of comprehension in his eyes.

"Yes, Philly — Zoya."

I went through it, step by step, for him. Marisa's birth mother, an empty, superficial woman, had sought solace from aging in the company of a younger, ruthless man. When that man no longer wanted her, she callously used her own daughter to extract revenge.

I still wondered about those deals of hers. She had once called Briachi "a pretentious lowlife." How could she have described him at all unless she was familiar with him and his home? It wouldn't surprise me to learn she collected a finder's fee on Hunt's arrangement with the mob. Maybe the blinding hatred she felt for her former lover wasn't exclusively personal in nature. It would explain why Hunt wanted the relationship kept quiet. A man who plastered his name on everything he touched didn't appear to have a consuming need for privacy.

"Hunt should have realized he was in trouble when Zoya agreed to sell him *at cost* the property he originally advised her to buy," I said in conclusion. "His charm sure hadn't prompted that generosity."

"I told you that you were good at this detective stuff," Philly muttered softly. He still looked stunned.

"Not good enough. My first inkling should have kicked in when I told her about Marisa's captivity. She slipped when she lamented that Marisa was being held in a 'cold building.' I thought she meant the weather, but she didn't. Why would she assume Marisa was being kept somewhere with no utilities?"

That was a mistake, yet I remembered that she covered it well. But telling me she was a dangerous woman, that was no mistake. Nor an error in an unfamiliar language. She was toying with me. How superior I felt when Weaver discussed his dream of returning to the South. I should not have felt above him. Everyone has illusions, and they always die hard. An enchanted five-year-old fan's had.

"She *was* a dangerous woman," I whispered, unaware that I had moved from thought to speech.

"Don't kid yourself, Tracy, Zoya loved danger."

True, I thought. After all her intricate planning, that she'd cut Belle's shooting so finely proved it. So much could have gone wrong. What if Hunt came early? Or if something blocked her escape? I wondered why she felt she had to silence Belle. Sure, Belle could have revealed the name of the "go-between" who set up the abduction. But she could have trusted Belle's loyalty to Hunt, if only Zoya was capable of trusting anyone.

I considered telling Philly about the shot Zoya fired at me, but I didn't want him to know that he was inadvertently responsible for it. He had already confirmed that when he picked up his pipe from her place, he told Zoya about our partnership. Still, that shooting haunted me. I could only guess at her motivation. When I first told her I was looking into the kidnapping, she tried to discourage me. She wanted the police to uncover evidence of Hunt's guilt. I bet she even hired her latest young lover to mug me so I wouldn't be able to continue. Zoya thought she had guaranteed police involvement by constructing a ransom demand the family would be unable to meet, since she held the missing share. What she hadn't counted on was the Eatons' predilection for denial.

When she realized the police weren't going to be brought in, she encouraged me to continue. I was her only hope. The shot fired outside the library was probably intended to make me angry enough to go on; she'd seen the way the mugging affected me. Then again, maybe she blamed me for keeping the police out of it. Who could say? I didn't believe she was trying to kill me. She was too good a shot; she proved that with Belle. But she didn't care if she had.

Philly broke into my thoughts. "Does Drew know the truth about Hunt?"

I shook my head. That might not be a thoroughly good idea. He should know the bond between his parents and his uncle wasn't as sinister as he feared. But if I shared that, how could I keep him from uncovering the rest of the story? Drew was a little too much Officer of the Court to handle this renegade justice. Someday, maybe.

"Weaver knows it wasn't Hunt, but he still wants to see him convicted," I said. "If he's even thought about who might be responsible, and I am sure he has, he hasn't said anything about it."

"Are you going to keep it quiet?" Philly asked.

I looked into the ballroom and watched as the Gypsy Princess threw her head back in happy laughter. Choked up myself, I nodded emphatically. Despite my disdain for secrets, I knew from now on I'd carry one, too, and I'd happily guard it for the rest of my life.

"What about Zoya?" Philly asked. "Do you care that she's getting away with it? I tried to reach her, but she left the country the day of the shooting."

"I'm not sure she's getting away with anything. Maybe your little story is right, Philly. The Gypsy Queen has been banished to a cold and empty place, because she carries it within her. Besides, those slow, grinding wheels of justice caught up with Hunt. Not to worry. Zoya's turn will come one day."

If I knew Weaver, he'd be watching for her the same as he did with Hunt. New York was Zoya's home; she wouldn't stay away forever. When he finally caught up with her, it would be on some matter that had nothing to do with Marisa.

"Sure it will," Philly agreed. He drew himself up and said with unexpected dignity, "Character is destiny."

Whoa! What a scary thought.

"You know, Philly, there's just one thing I haven't figured out." When I shivered, Philly removed his evening jacket, draped it over my shoulders, and pulled me close to him.

"What's that, sleuth?"

I explained how Weaver picked me up the day I followed him, and that Weaver believed Philly was planning a major scam against Lord Hunt. "You weren't, were you?"

"Nah, too uptown for my taste."

"Then where did he get that idea?"

"I called that tip in myself," Philly said through a sheepish grin.

"*You* did? Why?"

"You gotta understand, kid, I don't always know what I'm going to do. But I wanted to be sure I didn't pull something before my little girl's wedding. I thought if I made it sound big enough, the cops would watch me, and I'd have to be good. I didn't know it was going to become inconvenient."

He didn't always know what he was going to do. How could you help but love him?

I enticed him back to the ballroom and waited until we rivaled Fred and Ginger before spilling the best part. The children of the man Belle was indicted for killing always blamed Hunt for their father's death, and they had established a ten thousand-dollar reward for anyone giving information that led to Hunt's arrest and conviction on any serious charge.

"You'll have to wait till he's convicted, but I told Jay Weaver to give them your name for the reward, Philly."

"You and Drew should share," he insisted, though only for an instant. "Tracy, this is so generous."

I accepted his praise, though I swear generosity played no part in my decision. I was just looking out for myself. After all, locking in that reward for Philly was the *only* chance I had of getting *my* hundred bucks back!

Who cared about money, anyway? I was a detective now. For real. It wasn't something I just lied about — I proved I could really do it. And with unusual style, if I do say so myself.

I floated from the dance floor in the glow of anticipation. I couldn't wait for my next case! There was no stopping me now. Okay, so maybe there were one or two details that I could have handled better in the course of solving Marisa's kidnapping. Next time, I'd be dazzling. And I'd cherish every moment of it.

A man on the hotel's staff rushed toward me. I'd noticed him when I arrived — since he parted his hair just over his ear and wrapped endless strands of hair over his bald head like a snug black sweater, how could I help it? But I couldn't imagine why he seemed hell-bent on reaching me. He looked so excited, the sweater quivered.

He stopped before me and slapped his own cheeks with his hands. "It's you, I know it! She described you perfectly."

"Who . . . ?"

His eyes traveled the length of my gown. "But you must have put on few pounds since she saw you last."

"Excuse me?"

That funny man plunged on as if I hadn't spoken. "Is Martha Collins really your mother?"

"Why?" I asked with caution.

"She's on the phone — she has to talk to you *now*." He grabbed my arm and pulled me along. "Hurry up. Miss Collins said to tell you it's a matter of life-and-death."

Life-and-death?

Oh shit!

ABOUT THE AUTHOR

Kris Neri is a well-established writer of short mystery fiction. She is the author of over 40 published short mystery stories. In "L.A. Justice," which appeared in the *Murder by Thirteen* anthology, she introduced the Tracy Eaton character to the public and won the coveted Derringer Award. Kris was awarded a second Derringer for her story, "Capital Justice," which was published in the premier issue of *Blue Murder Magazine*. She lives in Southern California with her husband, Joe, and their "fur people," Morgan, Jake and Amanda.